MOS
LABS

Definitive Edition:
March 2023

ACT ONE OF
BLACK DIME CABARET

NEFARIOUS
SCHEMES
TO
MURDER
LADY
MIDNIGHT

a MOS LABS novella

A devastating plague grips France 1893, while a tumultuous election campaign dominates the headlines. An impressionable young woman arrives in the small town of Bellvoir with nothing but a letter of inheritance, handed to her by a mysterious clown.

In the gutter, rats feast on the sick, and the sick feast on promises of salvation from the enigmatic Raven Man. The famous Black Dime Cabaret, a haven for witches, opens it maws to the folk of the town who are oblivious to the secrets it contains.

And presiding over all, the most beautiful and feared woman in all of France: Lady Midnight.

CONTENTS

PREFACE

This novella is based on *Nefarious Schemes to Murder Lady Midnight*, the debut album from Black Dime Cabaret—a band which I am a part of. It's not written as a book that's meant to go out for publication to general audiences. It's odd, and controversially-written in regards to the traditional rules of storytelling; that is, I'm breaking them on every page. With that said, the book is the book, and you don't need prior knowledge of the music, or nineteenth century France, or literally anything, to enjoy it. It stands very much on its own.

To clear up any confusion, there are several other versions of this book floating around. They are all very similar, and in fact you'd be hard-pressed to find much difference at all. This version has only one notable modification: a few sentences gone from a single scene. It does nothing to alter the characters, lore or storyline, and if you haven't read either of the previous versions, then you're not missing out on anything.

The version you are holding now is the definitive version of *Nefarious Schemes to Murder Lady Midnight*, as far as I'm concerned. It's one hundred percent "canon" in the scope of the Black Dime Cabaret universe. This is the one true edition.

As I hinted at earlier, *Nefarious Schemes* is not much in terms of *fine literature*. It's a head-hopping, fluid-omniscient viewpoint orgy of characters, ideas and events that's my attempt at cramming as much information as possible into the most dense cake you've ever eaten. What the book does is it reveals and expands on our album in every way imaginable, to the extent you're probably justified in calling it gratuitous and over-the-top. That's the point. It's excessive, detailed, dizzying, and it's a world that I thoroughly enjoyed writing in.

I wrote this way back in 2019, over a very short period of time. The ideas were raw and spilled out of me rapid-fire in a matter of weeks. It was, above all, just a hell of a time. I'm excited to call this the definitive story, and to share it with as many people as possible.

If you enjoy it, please check out our band Black Dime Cabaret (as of the writing of this preface, we are just about to release our first big single, "The Clown and the Election"). We are a rock-pop-theatre fusion band using concept albums to tell a narrative over multiple albums, and it's a lot of fun.

Now, crack it open and welcome to the show!

Brandon
February 25, 2023

I

A Bad Case of Ravens

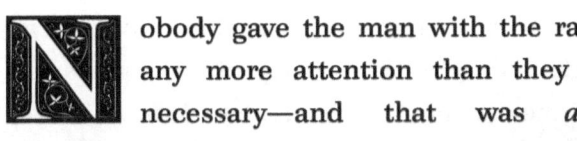 obody gave the man with the raven face any more attention than they deemed necessary—and that was *absolutely* necessary, which was to say: not much attention at all.

Not the ale-soaked drunkards who stumbled from those dingy street taverns, slicking the cobblestones with alcohol, singing atonal tunes about love affairs and ghosts. Not the crows that lined the eaves, chirping at the clouds, and taking flight into the starry sky.

A boisterous cheer came from way, way down in the dark of Bellvoir's lower districts, but you couldn't tell if they were cheering more drinks, more women, or more fights. It was obvious that those men took no notice of the man with the raven face, no more than they did the soggy leaflets and autumn leaves that tumbled across the wet cobblestones.

If flames had eyes, they would have spotted the man as they touched him ever-so-slightly with their warm amber hands, but even that was only the very *gentlest* touch.

Down an alleyway now, where the waifs and poor folk cuddled, breaths evaporating in white sheets of mist. Wide pupils and dirty faces stared up at the man with the raven face. One of them had only just turned three but nobody knew, because nobody in the gutter had the means to know nor celebrate birthdays. This child's older brother, a boy of nine years old and no name except the one scratched into his arm (Imbécile), stared at the passing raven man.

Is he from the theatre? the boy called Imbécile wondered, noting the man's raven mask, which covered his entire head and even some of his shoulders, black feathers draping him like a very expensive and frightening shawl. He found himself clutching his younger brother tighter.

The raven man did see the boy, but stopped only when he was past him.

He had long grown used to the sights and sounds

of a town that had offered its hapless weak to the festering rats. The politicians called it one of two things: a horrible epidemic or a hoax, depending on what resulted in the most votes. But the common thing nowadays was that it was a hoax. That the emaciated men and women grovelling at his feet were perhaps theatre performers, the blood and dirt makeup, the tears and stench and filth and broken voices and vomit and shit all just an old-fashioned show!

A rat squeaked by his foot and the raven man stomped on it before one of the women, naked but for roughly three layers of grime, could grab it for supper. The woman screamed, snatching the raven man's ankle and trying to peel the crushed rat from his soles. Its tail was still twitching. The raven man did not look at it and he was doubly glad not to when the woman began scooping mushed rat off his boot.

Somewhere behind him, near the entrance to the lower district, a gated door shrieked open and yellow light drooled out of a brothel. A prostitute stepped out to smoke a cigarette and she glanced down the alleyway towards the raven man, imagining he was one of those religious zealots who decided to prove their faith by sleeping with the rats and waking up without plague in their lungs. The next thing she thought was: who was to say there was a plague at all?

The raven man looked around at the grovelling poor. They would all be dead by the end of autumn but likely far sooner—he sure hoped it was sooner. The plague had a mind of its own, twisted and disturbed.

From his pouch he retrieved two loaves of bread, stale but a filling meal, and handed them to the woman who had been eating the mushed rat. Her dark eyes lit up as she took it in her trembling, blood-soaked hands. At first she was timid (last time a smirking man with a funny lion mask had given them mouldy bread that killed her sister), but the bread smelt good. With haste she unwrapped it and smashed it into her face.

The raven man watched the others swarm her. "There is some for everybody," he said, throat dry. He had not spoken all night. His voice was slightly muffled underneath the mask but he had always had a stronger voice than most, so it balanced out. The raven man's mother had been a famous opera singer. His father had been a wartime drill sergeant.

He unclipped a water bottle from his belt and handed it to the nine-year-old boy who had been watching him earlier. The raven man knelt, looking into the young boy's eyes, who took the bottle. It was only thirty years ago that the raven man had been that very boy, cold and hungry and frightened in the gutter without anybody—not even a little brother to take care of.

The raven man looked at the name on the boy's arm. Imbécile.

He withdrew a small glass inkwell from his coat pocket and dipped his finger into it, feeling the cold ink coalesce across his fingertip. He wrote over the name. REGIS. It was his own name. It had been his father's name before him. The name had power to it, and for as long as that boy had his name too, somehow the raven man knew he would be all right.

"Thank you," the little boy whispered, yet wondering why the man wore that raven mask. The boy could not see anything behind those glassy raven eyes.

Regis touched the boy's cheek. His skin was very soft, and very cold, even through gloves. He did not appear to be sick but his younger brother breathed like there was ink in his lungs. Exhaling sharply, Regis stood back up. "They will come through tonight and douse this place in fire. You'd best leave if you are well."

The boy who was once known simply as Imbécile stared at the raven man as he turned around and left, leaving a light dusting of feathers in his wake. A dark cape flapped behind him, drifting across the cobbles and infected.

The boy wondered where he had seen him before.

Regis hugged his large black coat tight about himself, righted his feathered shoulders, and did not look back. The raven mask was not uncomfortable. It was handmade with very real raven feathers, stitched together by the seamstress, Louisa. Those who saw it quivered in fear but none truly feared the man who left scraps for the dying.

There was a small shop way down in the lower district of Bellvoir, where two metal dice above the doorframe rung out sharply each time a new visitor entered—which was to say not often, for nobody but those seeking something very specific came to Ernest's shop.

Regis squeezed through the doorway, his head clinking against the dice as he passed the threshold and shut the door behind him. Dust jumped from the walls and gently fell. Moonlight slithered through cracks in the rafters and illuminated the dull, single room. The man at the other end of the shop, Ernest, peered up between the rows of shelves filled with newspapers and magazines and stale homemade snacks. He was a diminutive man with sallow skin and sunken cheeks that he desperately tried to cover with a beard, but the only sizeable growth on his face was a bulbous, black wart that occasionally made clicking sounds. He had always been an honest man in a dreadfully dishonest line of work, and his honest first thought when the door swung open and the twin dice rang was: *I really should have worn pants today.*

His second thought, upon seeing the man's raven face, the feathers streaking down his shoulders like a demented shawl, the large black coat, the place inside that coat which was large enough to conceal a weapon of devastating sorts, was: *Oh fuck.*

The dusty, wooden floorboards creaked as Regis walked between the shelves to Ernest. A small flame burned from a crooked wick at the edge of his wooden table, and beside it was a newspaper open to the headline: CANDIDATE BRUNO CHAPUT DROPS OUT OF ELECTION RACE TWO HOURS AFTER NEW ALLEGATIONS SURFACE.

"Praise the Raven," Ernest muttered.

"It is praised," Regis said curtly as he reached the table. From his coat pocket he withdrew a bag of coins and tossed it down by Ernest's flickering candle. It landed with a thud, knocking the candle aside, reflective coins spilling out onto the tabletop. Ernest stared at the cotton bag with ink-black eyes, no sign of white inside them. Regis observed the faint black feathers that scorched the side of the skinny man's neck, barely distinguishable in the darkness.

Red fire burned in the coins.

Ernest felt bile rising to his throat. "Is this everything?" His voice was pathetic, a whimper that seemed no louder than the gasps of those sick vermin out in the gutter.

Regis noted the man's obvious fear. "Calm down. All is well."

"Are you really going to kill her?" Ernest whispered.

"Think not of the act of murder," Regis said, "and more of what it means for the town. This plague will get us all if we do not remove the strain. It all stems from her. Remember that." He paused now, perhaps for dramatic effect. "You *must* remember that."

Ernest nodded without making eye contact—not that he would be making eye contact at all. Those were not Regis's eyes. Slowly, Ernest opened the desk drawer and pulled out a black dagger, its blade curved and engraved with emerald runes. The dagger ran the length of his forearm but it was incredibly light. It had not been an easy acquisition.

It passed the air between them, ending up in Regis's hands.

"Thank you for acquiring this for me," Regis said. "You have done well." He studied the gleam of the firelight against the edge of the dagger. It was a beautiful piece.

Ernest shivered. He had to do something. If Regis was to carry out his nefarious plan—murder the most dangerous woman in France—the consequences of doing such a thing would be catastrophic. Everybody knew this. The woman was unkillable, but she would remember it, and she would know that Ernest helped.

You're the only one who can stop this, Ernest thought.

From underneath the tabletop he felt the cold brass of his pistol. Bullets were expensive so he only had one barrel's worth and had used half of them guarding his shop from thieves, but Ernest knew from experience that it took only one calculated shot to kill a man.

Unfortunately, he was not good at this.

Sliding the dagger into his sheathe, Regis noticed Ernest move his hand underneath the table and immediately knew he was feeling for the pistol he had concealed there.

You don't want to do that, Regis thought.

Ernest thought, *I have to do this.*

Don't try it, Regis thought.

Ernest thought, *I should never have gotten involved with him.*

"Be calm," Regis said, his tone kind enough to

make Ernest loosen his grip on the concealed pistol, but not by much. "Your heroic deeds will be etched in French history forever." Regis slid his hand into the folds of his coat and pretended to touch a weapon of his own, knowing very well that Ernest feared him coming into his shop armed, knowing very well that Ernest didn't fancy himself much of a good shot and that he'd be easily outgunned.

"It wasn't easy," Ernest said with a tremor in his voice.

"A weapon of this calibre. I wouldn't think so. Well done."

"I . . ." He wet his lips. "I think, perhaps, you should pay me double."

"It will be as we agreed," Regis said. The coins on the table amounted to thirteen hundred francs, enough to keep a poor man fed for a considerable length of time in this year of 1893.

Ernest thought about this for a moment, but found himself unable to bargain with the man with the raven face, so he released the pistol and grabbed his nervous hands. They were full of sweat. He wouldn't have been able to carry the pistol at all.

"As we agreed, then." Ernest's voice cracked.

"You are always welcome among the Ravens," Regis said. He removed his hand from his coat and then patted it down pointedly, offering Ernest a smile underneath his mask.

"What's going to happen to me?" Ernest said.

Regis smiled. "My friend, once this is over you'll be free to do whatever you dream of."

I'll be dead if he tries to murder Lady Midnight, Ernest thought with dread, knowing that he would be unable to stop them, that the town would surely fall apart.

Regis took one step back. "The Raven smiles on you tonight."

And with that, he turned and walked out of the shop.

II

THE INHERITANCE

eventy-eight years ago, a message was scribbled on a tear of paper in expensive black ink. Once dry, the letter was folded in half once, twice, three times, and then small thin hands slid it into an envelope. The envelope was sealed with a blood-red stamp of a powerful family crest.

The man who wrote that letter was a young scribe by the name of Jacques, who was unfortunately murdered several months later—though, sure enough the murder was covered up and nobody cared enough to investigate. So he would be forgotten in time, the details of his life blurred and twisted beyond repair.

The man who dictated those words to Jacques, however, was none other than Count Lucien, suitor to all who crossed his path.

Lucien wore red on the night he was murdered.

He was standing on the third floor balcony of his much-lauded and respected estate, one so grand that it drew the eyes of every peasant and wealthy-man alike who so happened to view it from a distance; and up close, they could hardly stop themselves from trying the doors. He appointed guards now, several of them. Lucien had never been one to place himself amongst the commonfolk, instead preferring quiet evenings at the theatre or even quieter ones in his labyrinthine mansion. Sometimes, as was the case on the night he died, he spent it with women.

The wench's name was Rosalie and she was attractive but not more attractive than the Count himself. The most powerful, most well-renowned man in all of Bellvoir should not be overshadowed by the plaything he chooses to sleep with. But she was pretty nonetheless, raven-haired and green-eyed with a slight dusting of freckles.

She was watching him from the bed, the coverlets draped across her naked flesh. Moonlight trickled in through the floor to ceiling window where he stood in that garish red gown. The Count was reading scattered newspaper clippings and Rosalie knew precisely the words they contained. She was, unbeknownst to the Count, conversational with those in the press.

The Count of Bellvoir has secrets, they would say. *Expose him.*

"They think me a tyrant," said the Count as he turned to her, his open gown revealing a chest full of thick black hair, wolf-like. He was a muscled man with scars from wartime weaponry and he wore a large black beard with confidence, but he did not intimidate her. In his hand was one of those newspaper articles. The page became translucent as the moonlight streamed through it. He began walking over to her. "I am no tyrant yet," he said. "Just a man who grows more tired by the day." He offered a warm smile and Rosalie smiled back at him without parting her bright red lips, slightly smudged.

"Why not become something more?" Rosalie breathed.

The Count burst into baritone laughter as he tore the article in half and sat down on the edge of the bed, wrapping his gown about himself. Rosalie climbed up from the covers and rested her hand on his large shoulder. She followed his somewhat troubled gaze to a spot in the darkness lit by a single candle. The flame moved like a belly dancer, illuminating a painting of two unfamiliar but beautiful people.

"I fear that I will die without an heir," said the Count.

"That would be a shame," Rosalie lied.

Lucien looked at the wench and felt as though she were being honest with him. She was strikingly different to the other women he invited inside his quarters, or was that the wine talking?

He did not know the wine was poisoned.

"Would you give me a child?" Lucien said, and those were his last words because the next forty seconds consisted of him dying so noisily that Rosalie had to muffle his face with a pillow.

Rosalie remained in his quarters for at least thirteen minutes, during which time she rummaged through his secret stash, removing a pouch containing approximately twenty thousand francs, and some jewels of an unknown worth. Stories say she wore one of those jewels out of the estate, one of them encrusted with a cracked ruby that had belonged to the Count's mother, but none could confirm one such jewel ever existed and it was never found.

Among the dead count's possessions was a sealed letter, which he had dictated to a scribe called Jacques two nights earlier while a different woman had been in his bed.

Rosalie burned the letter.

Twenty-seven years later, in the year 1842, a young ballerina by the name of Antoinette would step out of the popular theatre in Paris, the *Théâtre de l'Odéon*, into a cold winter's night. A horse-drawn omnibus rattled past and she signalled for the driver to stop for her, but he did not, simply averted his weary sunken eyes and carried on, off and away down the snow-capped road. Antoinette clutched her fur linings tight and kept her head down.

The Paris nightlife swelled around her. Live music from bars, giggling girls and chattering men parading down the streets in very nice and sometimes extravagant outfits, lights from automobiles flashing along brick buildings. Antoinette danced lithely to the side as one screamed past, and she thought about all the ways a woman could murder her husband and get away with it.

"Whore!" he would scream at her, slamming her into the kitchen sink with one of his demented, putrid hands. Their kitchen was small but Antoinette had turned it into the prettiest kitchen in all of Paris, with beautiful pink flowers and open windows that gazed dreamily across the city skyline. This is what would happen:

She would grab a knife from the kitchen sink and throw it into his face and then he would give a blood-curdling scream and she would toss his body into the canal so that a fisherman fished him out and she could see his bloated, disgusting face one more time, and call him the ugliest piece of shit she had ever seen. And spit on him too.

Once he had tried to rape her after she had been awarded the best up-and-coming ballet dancer in Paris and she had used an iron to cook half of his face. She smiled to herself, recalling how it had gotten stuck to his skin and he had cried and wept like a baby.

He had told his friends he burnt himself working on the automobiles because he would never admit that he beat up his wife and got what he deserved.

Antoinette noticed a man watching her from underneath a street lamp just off the path. Light glinted off his small, round spectacles and she found herself somewhat drawn to him. The man wore a black suit and was thin, boyish-looking, but taller than most.

The man handed her a sealed envelope and said,

"You are the bastard daughter of Count Lucien and he would've liked me to have given you this."

Antoinette eyed the letter but did not take it.

"You have the claim to a beautiful estate in Bellvoir," the man who had no name told her, his voice soft and difficult to hear over the falling snow, "along with all of his possessions and wealth—and, do believe me, he was a wealthy man for the time."

"Why should I believe a word you say?" she asked.

"I was the only one who ever really knew your father and if you cannot take my word for it, then you will live the rest of your life knowing nothing about him at all."

Antoinette did take the letter but did not open it. Her husband left her six days after she spoke to the mysterious man and thus she did not get her wish of murdering him. She remarried at thirty and had two children, one of which died young. It was only on her deathbed, at age fifty three, that she remembered the letter.

And so it fell to Geneviève.

Geneviève loved two things in life: pottery and her husband, the thoroughly energetic and brilliantly charismatic Maurice. Maurice also loved two things in life: comedy and his wife. They lived in a small but beautiful house in the Paris neighbourhoods, having inherited a comfortable fortune from Antoinette, who was a world-renowned ballerina. They married young but they were dreadfully smitten.

War broke out in 1870. They would call it the worst war that ever came to France until the next war, and by then it had been thoroughly forgotten.

"I will always love you, my Geneviève," said Maurice, and those were his final words to her, because then he left to fight on the western front and that was the end of it.

At age nineteen, Geneviève was already pregnant with her first and only child. She died shortly after giving birth but lived long enough to see her daughter's cerulean eyes and her soft smile. She called her Celeste because her eyes looked like the universe and she knew Celeste would one day grow up to do wonderful things.

But their family wealth burned down in flames and Celeste was sold to the street rats. Her only company was a scandalous old leatherbound diary that had belonged to her grandmother, Antoinette, which she read up until thirteen when it slipped from her hands into a river.

War returned to France in 1887 and there she became a nurse, just sixteen years old but she lied about her age and growing up in the gutter put years on her. She had a way with healing people. The army did not pay well but it was enough that she did not have to sleep in the streets.

She did not like to think much about what happened there.

She was twenty-two when it ended, with little money.

And then the circus came to town. Celeste walked through the town square, watching the way the multi-coloured balloons danced in the wind. Evening sunlight streamed across the road like water and she tried to step from cobble to cobble, avoiding the cracks. She clutched her pink skirt as it flapped about her legs so as not to become tangled.

Celeste noticed a man watching her from underneath a cloud of balloons just off the town square. Light glinted off his pale makeup and bright red nose, and he had all the makings of a clown from the circus, except something about him seemed . . . *off*. Nobody moved towards him, in fact they seemed to pointedly avoid him. Yet she found herself somewhat drawn to him. The clown wore a red coat over a yellow button-up shirt, with a green handkerchief poking out of his shirt pocket. He was thin, boyish-looking, but taller than most.

The clown handed her a sealed envelope.

And so she came to be on a train as it pulled into the station of Bellvoir. She woke to an alarming screech, flung open the curtain beside her, letting in sunrays. It was five days since that conversation with the clown, the evening after a mysterious transaction took place in a dark shop in the lower districts, and the clown's words still flickered about her head.

"You have the claim to a beautiful estate in Bellvoir, along with all of his possessions and wealth—and, do believe me, he was a wealthy man for the time."

She had never gotten his name and sometimes she wondered if she had ever really seen him there at all. Only upon taking out that letter, and seeing the hastily-scribbled words inside them, did her mind even entertain the thought that it had actually happened.

Surely there is nothing left there, she thought. And it was a very valid one, she imagined, as the words in that letter must have been at least seventy years old, and on the back of two long and terrible wars, and she had not even heard of Bellvoir before.

She walked off the train with a single fraying bag containing everything she owned. She was the only one who did. Before she knew it, the train was leaving the station again, sending up a plume of autumn leaves in its wake. She squinted, watching it until she could see it no longer.

And then she was alone.

Wind howled through the maple trees, leaves skittered along the ground. A large, crooked clock hung from a brick wall leading out of the station. It read six o'clock in the evening, but that much was evident just by a glance into the amber sky, no clouds in sight. A raven flew overhead and Celeste followed it with her eyes, over the empty ticket booth and into the town proper, where it disappeared.

Bellvoir seemed like an ordinary town. It consisted of a very large and prominent main road, which coursed between lots of tall concrete buildings, many of them flavoured with shades of red but each one slightly different to the next, windows looking into small living rooms where couples danced to soothing records and children waved to passing pedestrians.

There was an abundance of trees, which Celeste was particularly fond of. Wartime was difficult but it was also long, and she had kept a sketchbook where she drew the trees and she asked the locals what they were called. She could name many of them just by glance. Bowl-like maples. A large and dominating sessile oak in a square of its own. She stood under a cork oak tree with its tangled roots creeping out of the cobbles, and smiled up into its canopy, spotting a white-beaked rook. It looked at her and she imagined that it smiled back.

"How are you?" she asked it.

"Bothered," she imagined it responding.

She frowned. "And why is that?"

"We don't like talking to . . . people. It conveys the impression that we are intelligent, where it would do us much better if all you common folk thought us dumb. That way we can get what we want which is, and why should I tell you this except for the fact you seem like someone a bird can trust, to one day murder everybody and rule this town."

"That sounds interesting," Celeste said.

The rook chirped. "Now quit bothering me."

A stray cat watched Celeste as she walked up the stairs into the immigration office on the corner of the main street (Muscat Street) and the street which led to the lake (Blanqui Street). The cat did not have a name but people liked to touch her, which annoyed her (she did not fancy people in general nor people touching her, especially after she had finished cleaning herself). Her only thought of the young girl in the pink dress was that she was a sorry sight.

"How may I help you?" asked the old bespectacled woman behind the immigration office counter. Celeste leaned into the glass divider and slid the letter from the clown across the wooden bench. The old lady, who looked like the kind of lady who works at the immigration office and holds immeasurable disdain for the world around her, sniffed loudly as if sniffing the letter. Celeste was sure that she was not sniffing the letter, but did not reject the hypothesis.

"I'm looking for the house at number six, Blanqui Street," Celeste said.

The woman peeled the letter from the counter and opened it up. Her small beady eyes flicked this way and that, seemingly reading the page out of order. Once done, she folded it back up and slid it over to Celeste. "I see. A cursed house, that one is."

And indeed it was. Hélène, who had spent the last forty years of her life behind that desk in the boiling hot immigration office, had seen many people come through. And all that time she had known that one day one of them would ask about the old house on Blanqui Street, the house that belonged to Count Lucien, who had committed suicide eighty years ago.

How is it that this girl came upon this note? she wondered, staring into the starry eyes of Celeste. Finding she had been staring too deeply into her eyes,

Hélène blinked and offered an inward smile—her face was unable to emote anymore.

"Sign here," the crooked lady said with disdain.

Celeste found a pen in her hand and the contract before her. She signed it and the house was hers. The stray cat watched her descend the stairs of the immigration office and pondered following her, but thought better of it. The girl had a bad aura about her.

The house at number six, Blanqui Street was situated at the foot of a large lake. Red leaves floated on the surface and the bank was muddy. A cobbled path circled the house, most of it broken with yellow grass. As for the house itself, Celeste could certainly imagine it had been a sight to behold once upon a time, with its three stories and eccentric architecture, the metalwork along the eaves shaped as birds and squirrels and other animals from the very mundane to the outright zany. But the place, for better or for worse, did not seem to have been touched in eighty very long years.

She threw open the large wooden doors. Light flooded across the vestibule, painting the tall wooden walls a bronze hue. Everything was overlarge and gaudy, and yet it did feel somewhat cosy. She let her bag slump to the floorboards and thought about how she would renovate it. Strip some of those paintings from the walls, give the floors a sweep.

Her eyes caught a chandelier on the second floor landing, unlit. All the windows were open and light streamed in, but it would soon grow dark.

A spider drifted down from the ceiling on the third floor. It passed the room where the old count had perished, not to suicide but from poisoned wine and a dangerous woman—the door now was ajar and it creaked in the breeze through the Count's open window. The spider had started in that room but had not been in there for twelve years. He perched briefly on the stairwell railing, peeking down at the girl who had entered. She had blonde hair which was the colour of webs when the setting sun shone through them.

From the railing, the spider swung to the second floor where he passed several guest rooms and he remembered how the house had once been something of a brothel full of lots of women. And the spider wondered how one man could have so many women at once. One year after the Count died, people stopped coming in and out of the house. Then the town had started to change. Roads were demolished and new ones built in their place.

The spider peered through a crack in the wall

between the second and first floor, at the lake. It had always been there but once there had been other roads, other houses. Now there were just parks and lots of empty space. This town was always changing, and oftentimes it was not for the better. But perhaps the spider just did not like change.

He watched the girl walk into the dining room, which was on the first floor. At that moment, he lost sight of her. *How annoying,* he thought, *that someone should return after all these years. Who does she think she is? Perhaps I should just kill her and be done with it.*

One second later a cat ate him.

Celeste heard a meow coming from the entrance. Cautious, she crept back that way and saw a black cat standing in a puddle of light, its green eyes watching her with judgment.

"Do you live here?" Celeste asked as she knelt before it.

The black cat brushed its head against her knee and walked in a circle around her, gliding against her back as it did so. Celeste gently patted its soft, springy fur, let the cat brush its jaw against the side of her hand. "Do you have a name, then?" she asked.

The cat meowed, emerald eyes flashing.

"Well, it's nice to meet you," Celeste said as she

got back to her feet, brushing cobwebs off her dress. She considered the cat. "I'll call you Nettie."

After her favourite grandmother, Antoinette.

Nettie brushed against her legs again and then wandered further into the house. Celeste watched her go, a smile on her lips. She grabbed her bag and then followed the cat, the floorboards creaking underneath her.

III

BLACK DIME CABARET

eleste woke early the next morning, her body wracked with pain. She cringed at the prickling sensation of insects in her lower back, as she pried herself to the edge of the bed. Morning light poured through the shuttered window behind her, and she contemplated the decision to sleep on that sunken mattress. Motes of dust shimmered in the sunlight and she watched them rap against the walls of her second floor bedroom. It was small but comfortable. At night, the only sound was the soft drawl of music, drifting from someplace unseen.

Rubbing the arch of her back, she slid off the bed

and slipped her feet into slippers before wandering to the window where she drew the curtain aside. Bellvoir opened up before her, its red mismatching buildings, the distant clock tower moments from nine o'clock. Mechanical automobiles rattled by her house and people walked in the streets. Dogs occasionally barked as they chased butterflies in the breeze and birds squawked from the maple trees.

She pictured her checklist, a scrap of paper she'd torn from her journal, scrawled with black ink. It consisted of many things, predominately food, supplies, new bedsheets, and a visit to the Black Dime Cabaret on the corner of Soupirs and Lilas Street, the place her great grandfather had mentioned in his initial letter to her. She could not make out that place from her window, but she could feel its presence there, a deep purr from within the town depths.

"What do you eat?" Celeste asked Nettie as she crossed the small second-floor landing between her bedroom and the bathroom. She bathed and pinned up her hair with moderate trouble, before dressing in a pale blue dress.

Celeste applied a little bit of makeup and then descended to the first floor. It was only then that she stopped and looked around. Something seemed different. Perhaps it was just her. Frowning, she walked to one of the paintings on the walls and touched it gently. Where previously the old-fashioned portrait had appeared cracked and aged, this morning the very same one looked like it could have been painted yesterday.

The walls, too, seemed less flaky. She adjusted her centre of gravity on the old wooden floorboards and they did not creak as they previously had.

Odd, Celeste thought.

Nettie meowed as she perched on the stairwell railing. Spotless and golden, it shone with what appeared to be a new coating of polish. Nettie, too, had taken note of how things had changed. There were less rats and less webbing in the cracks. As the girl called Celeste made for the front door, Nettie strolled about the vestibule, watching her with interest. Who was she really and why had she come here?

An autumn leaf tore from the highest branch of an old oak tree and streaked through the early morning sky. It leapt over the spire of the clock tower, which tolled nine o'clock, and then streamed down by the church where a moderate crowd was gathering. Bellvoir was a town designed with no clear regard for artistic style. It was nothing more than a scattering of roads and mismatching buildings, and it only got worse each time a new man found himself in power. Buildings were torn down, streets redesigned, to fit the new mayor's own preference. It was clear, from the leaf's point of view, that none had ever seen the town from above, for if they had they would most certainly be disgusted by the mess it truly was.

The wind picked up and the leaf was tossed up and about, floating serenely by a wooden signpost with three arrows attached to it. There was the inn called the *Cormorant* and standing there in the centre of the crossroads was a man handing out election pamphlets.

"Vote for Mathieu," he said in a somewhat unenthused voice as a woman brushed past him, purposely avoiding eye contact. The man's name was Theo and, to be honest, *he* probably wouldn't even vote for his father except that he had no choice—and the other candidates weren't so much better.

"Do you want new roads?" Theo said to a man who had a cane and a very nice top hat. He wanted to ask where he got the hat but the man quickened his pace. *He probably votes for Anatole's lot,* Theo thought, because all the businessmen liked Anatole's proposed policies. They were good for the economy, especially in these unstable times. You could still smell the embers of the war. It smelt like poverty, recession and plague.

"Gustave Mathieu supports women," Theo said, proffering a pamphlet to a young blonde-haired girl who was walking past. The girl stopped and looked at the pamphlet. He shook it towards her. "Have you made up your mind?"

Celeste looked at the man with curiosity. He was a young man with a decent fashion sense but quite plain in all other aspects. "Regarding what?" she asked.

"Well you have to vote for *someone*."

Celeste pictured her checklist. Casting a vote in some election was not on that list. And yet she felt somewhat intrigued. Pursing her lips, she said, "Who are my options?"

Theo cringed. *My job is to hand out pamphlets,* he thought. *Not talk to you about all the political candidates, several of which I am completely uneducated on.*

He faked a smile. "Well I would say to vote for Mathieu but perhaps I am a little biased." He rapped a finger against the many blue pins he wore across his coat. "There's Julien Lémieux who's somewhat of a shady man campaigning for the expansion of the town. He's popular but shady. Folk like Colette and

Horace who want mostly the same thing, which is the imminent destruction of France. Of course—"

"Okay," Celeste said politely. "I get it now."

Theo choked on his words. "Oh. I'm sorry."

"I have to go." Celeste smiled, tore one of the pamphlets from his hand and took off down the street, Theo watching her until she was out of sight.

IN THE THIRD FLOOR OF THE BUILDING ACROSS THE road, a man watched them from his window smoking a pipe. He wore a red dress coat and the room itself was also deeply red. Chequered sunlight illuminated his mottled skin, only partly repaired by a thin layer of makeup. The hem of his long red coat had snared the edge of his wooden desk. A globe of the world lay still, South Africa facing the chandelier on the ceiling. A nameplate read FERDINAND ROUSSEAU.

"That there is Theo Mathieu, Gustave's boy," Ferdinand said. "How pathetic. Gustave and his miserable lot truly are doomed, now resorting to that tool of a boy." Gustave put an awful lot of faith in that boy, his only son and likely successor to the cause. Ferdinand figured a good way of stopping the movement in its tracks was eliminate the boy.

He smirked to himself as he turned from the window and faced the rest of the room, very red and very expensive. Some might call it gaudy but Ferdinand simply liked it. He wasn't trying to prove a point or display his wealth, it was just how he was.

Standing by the door in front of a portrait of himself was Zoé, her dark hair twisted up in a showy piece, the same shade as her eyes and her freckled skin. There was also a man reclined on the single-seater couch in the corner, one leg folded over the other, expensive brand-name brown shoe on display, and a newspaper in his lap. His name was Laurent and he didn't say much, preferring to observe, but he was the smartest man in France and when you were in the same room as Laurent, you felt like you could do anything.

Laurent was staring at the opposition leader over his newspaper, tilting his spectacles down onto the very tip of his nose. Ferdinand was his key to everything in France. The inner circles of high society, the power. The meetings. The parties. The *men*. That was not to say he did not appreciate Ferdinand personally—the two had miraculously remained friends since childhood, where most of Ferdinand's childhood friends were dead, having perished in the wars, or, in some other cases, "accidents." Laurent did know that Ferdinand was not as bad as they said.

"I need you," Ferdinand had told him frequently. "I want France. You want what comes with France. Let's work together, and when we get what we want, let's split the riches."

Laurent was sure they would.

Zoé decided she had walked into the opposition leader's office at an inopportune time but it was too late to leave. Once Ferdinand latched onto you, he didn't let go. And so there she was, standing just inside the doorway, feeling like she should run. She was nobody of any significance but she had heard stories about the man. That he liked to abuse his power.

So Zoé kept still and tried not to look at anything in particular. Maybe he wasn't as bad as they said. She had never had anything bad happen to her in particular, and Ferdinand *had* given her a chance here when others wanted her deported. So perhaps it was stress over nothing?

Ferdinand was eyeing her hard, his eyes blue and exuberant.

Zoé felt a shiver run from her spine through her shoulders.

Laurent returned to his newspaper and turned the page to the forecast.

"Please, do come inside," Ferdinand said, motioning to her. Zoé said nothing, just walked forward into the eloquent, pretentious room. She held her breath, glancing over at the man on the white couch. He met her eyes for a tiny moment. She looked away, heart racing. There was something off about that man. Ferdinand smiled softly at her and slipped the letter out from between her fingertips, promptly opening it up and taking a look.

Oh, it's the polling numbers, he thought to himself. He only needed to see their own numbers to know it wasn't looking good. They had been far behind when the campaign started and, tens of thousands of francs later they were still very far behind. He folded it up and handed it back to her. "The polling numbers are always fabricated. Just more propaganda from Archambault."

Laurent raised a brow at this but said nothing.

Ferdinand weighed her up. She tensed under his hot gaze and tried not to move. He sensed her apprehension and immediately withdrew, collecting a letter from his pocket and handing it to her. "See that this is delivered to the immigration office."

Zoé took the letter and left, Ferdinand watching her.

Only then did Laurent lower his newspaper and

prop his spectacles back before his eyes. He waited until Ferdinand looked at him, which meant he was out of options. "If I may," Laurent said in a calm voice—always calm. "The polls do not look good. Say what you will, but the numbers are not falling in our favour and come time to vote we will need nothing short of a miracle to get us over the line. With that being said, I do foresee another road to power in the form of one Lady Eleanor Beaumont."

"Lady Midnight," Ferdinand said.

"Let's not go around calling names." He did not know where the names came from but he did not concern himself with public judgment. It was meaningless what they thought. "I think you should meet with her to discuss a partnership."

Ferdinand visibly quivered at the proposal.

Laurent sensed this. "Or I can meet with her."

"They say she is a witch," Ferdinand said. He did not like this idea at all, and yet when had Laurent ever proposed something that did not work out? He ran a hand through his long brown hair and then grabbed his chiselled jawline. "She is an elusive woman."

"You are the wealthiest man in France."

"That is not exactly true."

"If excuses and ignorance are your defences," Laurent said with dismissal, reclining in the couch and raising the newspaper to his eyes, "there is nothing I can say to convince you. Except that Lady Beaumont is a dangerous woman and she likely wants you dead."

"Wants me dead?" Ferdinand blurted out.

"You're taking votes from her every day."

"Oh, then murdering me makes perfect sense."

"You're both after similar things; Lady Beaumont is just better at telling that to the people. An alliance will benefit you both. However, it will be easy to convince her that it will benefit her more."

"It does sound like it will, though," Ferdinand said.

Laurent smiled. "Of course it does."

Ferdinand did not like this one bit.

"I hear she has an establishment on the corner of Soupirs and Lilas Street that more than one candidate is threatening to demolish. You have the funds to save it." He peered up over the top of the newspaper. "Funds that might buy you into her inner circle of trust."

The Black Dime Cabaret, Ferdinand thought.

Then he asked, "What makes you think this ends with an election victory for us?"

"Look around you, Ferdinand. The plague. The death. Everybody's scared, everybody's looking for someone to blame. There's a lot of misinformation going around, a lot of lies, but all that matters is that some lies are easier to believe than others. There is a stick of dynamite in this town that is threatening to explode and, when that happens, think of where the pieces lie. In the end, and most importantly in the eyes of the people of Bellvoir, there is one witch in this alliance and one wealthy, powerful man with a chance to be the hero."

Ferdinand smiled in earnest for the first time that day.

THERE WAS A LARGE BLACK BUILDING ON THE corner of Soupirs and Lilas Street, with red windows and classical architecture that made it stand out from every other building in Bellvoir. The entry was a crimson door underneath a sign which read: BLACK DIME CABARET.

Celeste looked up at it, feeling a sense of . . . familiarity. Outside the stark black establishment, skeletal autumn trees stood like scarecrows, their amber leaves drifting about the cobbled roads. An elderly man in a grey coat and a striped top hat stopped beneath one of these trees as he walked his dog, cane in one hand, leash in the other. He glanced up at the heights of the Black Dime establishment, visibly shivered, and then walked on without looking back.

"To my one true heir," Count Lucien dictated to his young scribe Jacques on a cold winter's night, "a claim is yours to the order of the Black Dime. There awaits you . . ." He paused and Jacques glanced up softly from the letter, in anticipation. Count Lucien lowered himself onto the edge of his bed and thought to himself. "There awaits you everything I have left."

Celeste carefully adjusted her purse and walked to the door. By all accounts this door seemed ordinary enough, vertically-pinned wood painted stark crimson, with a metal handle. She grasped the handle and pushed the door open.

Soft cabaret music and a hot pink light trickled out of the Black Dime Cabaret as Celeste stepped inside, closing the door behind her. A coat rack stood to her immediate left, currently holding several fine coats and one top hat. To her right, a woman with pale makeup and red swirls on her plump cheeks smiled at her from behind a bar where two men in costume drank.

That music was coming from some place beyond

three descending steps, past the tables and chairs, from a slightly-elevated stage where a woman sung a quiet song to a barebones audience. At one of the tables as far back from the stage as you could sit, a young woman was sketching in an overlarge book.

Celeste imagined how the place would look with more people. It seemed that doors and hidden passages in the walls led deeper into the establishment but you really needed to look hard to see them. Eyes were drawn instead to the paintings on the walls, the soft purple lights, the people who loitered in the shadows all in costume.

"Hello, hun."

Celeste was spun around by the hand of a woman wearing a venetian masquerade mask. She jumped, taking a step back. The woman lowered the mask to reveal a pretty, made-up face with strawberry blonde hair cut atypically before her shoulders. She wore a black corset that highlighted the paleness of her skin, which had an almost marmoreal look about it, waxy and fake.

"I am so sorry!" the woman blurted, grabbing Celeste's hands in her own and cackling under the pink lights. She released her and then stood there, doll-like, her neck slightly cocked forward, shoulders slumped as her arms hung lifelessly by her sides.

"I'm Léa. Are you here for the show or are you after something else?"

"Show?" Celeste asked.

"The matinee," the woman called Léa said.

"Oh, no," she spluttered, withdrawing the letter from her great grandfather and sliding it into Léa's hand. "I'm just here because of this letter. My name is Celeste. I think... Count Lucien was my great grandfather."

Léa's façade changed immediately. She regarded the letter with suspicion, then regarded Celeste. She flipped open the letter and scanned it with incredible speed.

"Marguerite," she said, striding from Celeste to the woman behind the bar, with the red whorls on her plump cheeks. Marguerite perked up her head. Celeste cautiously followed Léa, trying to ignore the nagging eyes of those other two performers, as one of them let out a breath of smoke and squashed down his cigarette in a fancy ashtray.

Léa threw the letter onto the bar as Celeste arrived. The shadows meowed. A cat was there, watching Celeste with one emerald eye, the other one yellow. It purred softly and did not take its eyes off her.

"She claims to be the great granddaughter of the Count," said Léa with what appeared to be mixed parts scepticism and intrigue. She occasionally glanced at Celeste, curious.

Marguerite picked up the letter with theatre and held it up to the light. One of the men at the bar, wearing a comically-tall purple hat decorated with stripes and a flower, borrowed a cigarette from his friend and said, "Can she dance?"

"We do need another dancer," said his friend offhandedly.

Léa leaned her forearm on one of the men's shoulders and let her fingers drum against her bright red lips. "*Can* you dance, darl?"

Celeste shrugged, looking between them. This place was so odd, she thought, and the people no less. But the piano music kept dreamily frolicking. The woman on-stage kept singing. The cat kept purring. The door opened and a tall woman walked in with heels in one hand, a purse in her other. She greeted everybody and Léa hugged her, kissing her on the cheeks. Then she was off and all eyes slumped on Celeste, who watched the woman until she was gone.

"I don't really dance," she said at last.

"A shame," said Léa as she raised her masquerade mask to her face. It covered the curve of her nose and upwards, leaving only her eyes and bright red lips.

She took one of the men's glasses and drank what was left of it as Marguerite returned the letter to her.

Marguerite was a spectacle. You could imagine her raven hair was long if she let it down, but she wore it in an immaculate headpiece full of curls and rolls. Celeste found herself staring at the red whorls on her cheeks, feeling herself be drawn into them. She immediately knew that Marguerite was not just the hostess; she was something very different.

"Come here, child," Marguerite said, indicating her to the bar.

Celeste found herself standing face-to-face with her, the men on her right, Léa on her left, Marguerite leaning forward across the bar, taking her chin in her hands.

"I see it now," Marguerite said. "Perhaps it's true." She released Celeste's chin and then poured her a glass of something red and bubbly. She slid it across the counter. "You have come to the right place, my dear. What is your name? Celeste?"

Celeste nodded, glancing at the drink.

"When did you arrive?" Marguerite asked.

"Yesterday," Celeste said with uncertainty. There was something strangely dulling about this place, even without the wine, that clouded her thoughts and made her want to forget things. It did something to her head. The music. The costumes. The stares.

"Where did you get this letter?" Marguerite asked.

Celeste thought about this for a moment. The town square. The balloons. The man who everybody avoided, everyone except her. "A . . . clown gave it to me." It all seemed so odd but the memory was blurred, like an aging vignette. Had it happened at all? Her hand flew out and took the conical glass, and she took one sip of it. Wine. Just wine.

Marguerite nodded thoughtfully. "Most curious. Come back tonight. Eleven, maybe? Find yourself a seat down at the stage. Aurélie is performing with her band."

Celeste smiled and nodded, but with apprehension. She glanced sidelong at the woman called Léa, who smiled back at her, raising a wine glass. "We would love to see you there," Léa said in a kind, sultry voice. "A night at the cabaret."

CELESTE WALKED BACK OUTSIDE, TRANCELIKE. SHE heard the door squeal as it shut behind her, clapping against the latch. Several blue kingfishers flocked from a skeletal tree overhead, disappearing over the brick buildings. Election papers tumbled along the cobblestones with orange autumn leaves.

She stared after them. Head over heels, drifting over a cracked cobble and changing direction right before slapping into a tree bole. And then they stopped, flopping to the ground and ending their journey at an overlarge, red shoe.

She looked up to see the face of a clown.

He was too far to make out clearly but she could not mistake him, standing under tree branches down the road, large red clown shoes, red coat over a yellow button-up shirt, with a green handkerchief poking out of his shirt pocket. Celeste gasped, goosebumps prickling her arms as the wind suddenly became very, very cold.

She is odd, the clown thought, staring at her from afar. His face itched underneath the makeup, hair twitching underneath the darned purple hair. Straightening his collar, he turned and walked off, letting the girl be. He wouldn't want to frighten her, just be there.

The clown was always there. Always watching.

He turned a corner and disappeared from sight.

IV

THE HOUSE OF ELEANOR BEAUMONT

ady Eleanor Beaumont, or Lady Midnight to those who feared her mysterious ways, lived in a lavish manor house in the wealthy part of Bellvoir.

Her manor house was the tallest building in the district, stark black and castle-like, with battlements and arrow slits in the towers. Red windows glared predatorily across the city, and when you looked up at it—from wherever you were in Bellvoir, even in the slums of the gutter—you would earnestly feel as though something was watching you.

Hubert Gros dropped to his knees on the burgundy carpet of Lady Beaumont's living chambers, his head bowed so low he could smell the faraway country they'd imported the carpet from. He was shaking, sweat dribbling from his brows. Hubert was not fat by any means, but the manor halls were twisted and long and his stamina was minimal.

"Quit grovelling," Lady Beaumont said, her voice so beautiful, so extraordinary that it made Hubert immediately obey her, the smell of everything pleasurable filling his nostrils, the taste of spring on his tongue. He looked up and was greeted not only by the poised, perfect figure of Lady Eleanor Beaumont but the church-like architecture of her chambers.

Massive, arched windows let out onto a twisted distortion of the town of Bellvoir, everything tinted red. The sun cast long shadows across the chamber between the mahogany pillars which lined every single wall. Near the rafters he met the eyes of gargoyles and other odd creatures that he would never dare to know the names of. But he was very close to believing that at least one of them was staring at him, drawing slow yet very alive breaths.

But not the classical architecture, the massive arched windows, the statues nor the late fourteenth-century renaissance paintings nor the lavish carpet held anything towards the beauty that was Lady Beaumont herself. She wore a black dress that blossomed about her feet, seeming to bristle in a breeze that could not possibly be there. It clung to her curvy, slender figure in all the right ways, statuesque. Her auburn hair glittered about her shoulders. In her hand she clutched a wine glass, half-full, and she sloshed it occasionally. Hubert watched in awe as the expensive, cultivated wine jumped up against the sides, hugging the lip.

Hubert brushed himself off as he rose to his feet.

Lady Beaumont slowly approached him. She was taller than he was, so graceful as she stepped, her raven dress parting every so often to reveal onyx heels. In the corner of his eye, Hubert spotted one of the fluffy red chairs blink at him. One of the gargoyles that perched upon a pillar let out a sigh and reclined. Hubert refocused his attention on Lady Beaumont, fighting the sudden urge to wipe sweat from his face.

He found himself trapped as the sun dipped at just the right angle, sending a wash of red light pouring in a single puddle across the chamber, illuminating Lady Beaumont, and him inside her magnificent, snake-like shadow.

"How charming you are," Lady Beaumont said as her plump red lips curved into a smile and she took his chin with her cold, cold fingertips. Hubert tensed, both at how cold her fingers were, like icicles, and then sensing her breath against his face as she peered down at him through rays of red light. Her eyelids were painted as black as the cosmos itself. Hubert thought only astronomers could see the stars and yet he saw them now, as she peered into his soul.

Lady Beaumont proceeded to walk around him, her soft dress brushing the side of his leg and sending shivers through his whole body. "Tell me what you've found," she breathed, standing behind him with her perfect, pale hands on his shoulders.

Hubert didn't dare move, his heart fluttering. "I did as you asked, my lady," he said, suddenly seeing a flash of the man in his mind's eye. His muscles spasmed and he heard the sound he'd heard that night, the sound of ravens screaming in horrible distress. "I followed the raven cult man down..." He paused, licking his lips. His stomach heaved. He would not say where exactly he followed the raven man.

As Lady Beaumont drew a sip from her wineglass and strolled from Hubert to one of the tall columns which lined the chamber, he continued, "He met with a man in a very dark, very unusual shop, and a transaction took place. There's a plan, Lady Beaumont."

He was back there now, standing outside the shop

with his ear to the wall, heartbeat drumming in his ears. He could hear the cries of the sick as they clawed at dead rats and sucked on infected meat. A biting wind hurtled down the alley, throwing open one of the wooden doors and then slamming it shut again. Hubert jumped, breathing heavy and fast.

"Are you really going to kill her?" one of the men inside the shop whispered. This was not the raven man. His voice was quiet and shaky, occasionally breaking. Hubert hoped the raven man didn't kill him, not right here. Hubert did not like murder at all.

"Think not of the act of murder," the raven man said, "and more of what it means for the town. This plague will get us all if we do not remove the strain. It all stems from her. Remember that." He paused—a very long and drawn-out pause. "You *must* remember that."

Oh god, Hubert thought as he shuffled away from the door and accidentally knocked his foot into a wooden bucket that some fool had left there. It crashed to the cobbles, clanking down the alleyway. Rats squawked and Hubert grabbed his mouth to stop himself from shrieking, his feet dancing to avoid touching any of the infected rats. He ran from the spot and never looked back.

Lady Beaumont stood still when he finished telling

her. Red light from the sun beyond her impressive arched windows shone across her marmoreal skin. He couldn't take his eyes off her, not even if he wanted to. "They would dare to murder me."

Hubert did not have a response to this.

Lady Beaumont looked at him. Something moved beyond her, in the spot she had just turned from. One of the gargoyles had disappeared—he was certain of it! And then there was a knocking at the window and he spotted an imp-like creature standing there, fully naked, smiling and waving at him. He forced himself to focus back on Lady Beaumont. He wiped his sweating palms on his pants. She stared at him but did not move closer.

"Where did you follow him to?" she asked.

He cleared his throat. "My lady—"

There was a horrifying scream from within the house of Eleanor Beaumont, which lasted approximately thirty seconds, a scream that sent birds flying from their nests and made a partially-deaf man on the street look up thinking he'd heard something. The scream was so loud, indeed, that nobody heard the creaking and snapping of bones that went along with it. And so it was that poor Hubert Gros died a painful and pathetic death on her carpeted floor with his elbow bone on the ground beside him and his spine hanging out, his left hand as twitchy in death as it was in life—not that Hubert ever had much of a life to speak of.

Lady Eleanor Beaumont descended the winding stairwell to the first floor where she placed her empty wine glass on a table and strolled out underneath a chandelier, feeling the warm fire tickle the hairs on the back of her neck.

"Guillaume," she called out.

A massive suit of armour stepped out from the shadows. Eleanor smiled as she approached it, craning her neck up to stare through the slats in his helmet, at the grotesque, zombie-like face inside it. Guillaume's breath stank like dead meat. He purred softly.

"There is a small shop in the lower districts where two metal dice hang above the doorframe," Eleanor said to him, gently brushing her hand against his rusted armour. "A man works there alone. Would you do me a favour and deal with him for me?"

Guillaume only knew one thing: he liked killing. The thought of it made him happy. Doing it brought him immense joy. Feeling a rush of anticipation, he grunted. Lady Beaumont leaned in and kissed him on the armour, leaving a print of her red lipstick.

"Thank you, Guillaume," she said.

Guillaume only knew one thing: murder.

So he walked out of the manor house and prepared to do some.

Eleanor watched him until he was gone, with the large wooden doors closing behind him. She breathed in the sweet scent of autumn air and turned on her heels, preparing to return to her chambers. The festival was starting tomorrow, and then the ball the following night. The grand ballroom of her manor house looked far too lonely right now.

But all she needed now was a bath and some wine.

ERNEST HAD PRECISELY NO CUSTOMERS THAT morning, but that was okay, he thought, sitting on the wooden chair behind the counter, because he was going to leave this place anyway. He stared at the open door, which swung in the breeze, the two dice ringing against each other. Autumn sunlight spilled through the alley, dripped through the rafters and tattered curtains into his shop. Motes of dust tumbled in the sunrays and he watched them, somewhat intrigued, while his hand turned the page of his morning newspaper.

A rat squawked as it scurried through a crack in

the floorboards, into the shop. It was a very small shop, and dark, and dusty, but comfortable. The rat sniffed loudly, its tiny head flickering about. It skirted a wooden shelf, dodged a ray of sunlight, and grabbed hold of a dead spider. The spider was crusty and dry as it lay on its back, legs folded in on itself.

The rat enjoyed the meal and then looked up, meeting the eyes of a man sitting on a chair. Ernest thought nothing of the rat, only that it was disgusting. He was already infected. The red-splattered handkerchief was crinkled on top of his table. His stomach was cramped but he'd been thus far unable to shit or throw up. For a brief second, his eyes touched the tall pile of coins nearby the handkerchief. His whole body grew hot.

He turned a page of his newspaper. *Family dies in house fire massacre,* he thought to himself as he scanned the article. *The husband and her three children, burned to death. Woman hangs herself in the stable. Everything's there except her feet.*

That was all France was nowadays. Death and despair. And to think now it had reached Bellvoir and soon he would be dead too. *How far will it spread from here?* He knew what Regis, king of the raven cult, wanted, and he figured that perhaps this country did need a change after all.

He turned the page and came face-to-face with Jean-Marie, whose circus came around every so often but not this fall, not with the whispers of plague. What did it matter anyway? *He's mildly unwell*, the article claimed, or something to that effect. He would be dead by the winter.

Sunlight glinted off the stack of coins on the table.

It was going to happen at the ball, two days from now. Regis was going to stroll straight through the doors into Lady Midnight's chambers and put a dagger through her heart. Ernest chuckled without mirth. Nobody could kill Lady Midnight—and they had certainly tried. He desperately wished he had never gotten involved in this, never risked his life (on multiple occasions) to procure that bloody dagger! But it was too late now. Ernest could do nothing, just wait for the eventual aftermath. The end of France.

Resting the newspaper on the table, he leaned forward and stared straight into those coins. Each individual coin seemed to cast its own light, but he knew that could not be the case. He wondered how exactly Regis had come upon all this fortune in the first place. Who *was* Regis? His fingers searched for the feathers that grew out of his neck, and scratched them. The itch was almost debilitating some days, his nails breaking flesh and drawing blood. In the coin reflections he saw his two black, beady eyes. He remembered the ritual. The curved knife that Regis had used to murder a raven and bleed it. And Ernest had drunk the blood. Coppery. Warm. Like soup.

And now he was praised by the Raven.

But also terribly alone, and frightened. They were all afraid but Ernest more than most. Somehow he had managed to make enemies of everybody. It was because he thought too much, became distrustful, doubted his own mind. Every tangent led to variations of the same thing: destruction of France. Lady Midnight and her plague. Regis and his raven cult. The politicians and their patrons, every goddamn person dead-set on making the worst decisions possible and destroying them all . . .

A massive shadow fell across the store.

Ernest looked up to see a giant fill the doorway, his metal head clanging against the two dice that hung there. Ernest sprang to his feet. The entire room was quiet except for metal footfalls as the giant walked inside, the autumn sunlight revealing a very rusted, very old suit of armour, which covered him from top to bottom.

Guillaume drew his sword and did not stop walking.

"You," was all Ernest said before he fumbled his

pistol from his coat and fired six times, the shop flashing theatrically. Nobody heard but the sick people grovelling in the alleyway outside, and a single disease-ridden rat, who darted into the shadows as a large, metal foot smashed down beside it.

"Get back!" Ernest screamed, throwing his pistol at the armoured monstrosity.

Guillaume watched it bounce off his chest plate, much like the bullets. He smelt the diseased meat of the shopkeeper, and it made him drool onto his rotten chin.

Ernest scooped up the coins and began tossing them at the metal giant one-by-one but they just rebounded with quiet *clinks*. He lifted the desk by one hand, flinging it maladroitly at the giant. Guillaume threw his shoulder into it, the table exploding into tiny shards which blasted across the room. Ernest screamed, stumbling backwards and cracking his head against the rear wall. A flash of white ripped through his vision.

In a nearby chapel, Regis sat upright. He was seated on a pew at the very back, away from the ceremony taking place. A christening. The baby had suddenly begun to cry as the priest sprinkled holy water over his pudgy, red face.

Something has happened, he thought, feeling a

sharp pain in his wrist. He pulled up his sleeve to reveal a burn of black feathers. His first thought was someone had been murdered. His second was that Ernest had done something and the mission was jeopardised.

He stood up sharply. The old man sitting in front of him looked warily over his shoulder, giving Regis an odd look. The grandfather of the child, perhaps, or just another stranger like himself. The old man muttered something to his wife, who wore a green dress with pink flowers patterned across it.

Regis turned and fled the chapel.

Guillaume towered over Ernest with his gigantic broadsword. He obscured the light, his rusted metal armour reflecting Ernest's frightened face as he raised his arm to block the monster's massive sword.

"Please don't kill me!" Ernest cried, spittle flying.

Guillaume raised his sword in two hands and then sunk it through Ernest's skull, splitting it in two. The body flopped to the ground. Blood dribbled from the edge of the blade, the sound of raindrops falling from the eaves after a horrible storm. A rat squeaked and darted from the shadows, fleeing the shop immediately.

Throwing open the doors of the chapel and striding out into the town square, Regis took in a deep breath and found himself staring up at the black manor house on top of the hill. The house of Eleanor Beaumont.

She knows about the plan, he thought.

Fear tugged at him, sending shivers through his body with such ferocity that he nearly collapsed there on the doorstep of the chapel. He sucked in another deep breath and tightened his coat, fighting the sudden drop in temperature. All the while he could not shake his eyes from the red arched windows of Eleanor Beaumont's estate. The sight was vile, horrid, insidious, yet terribly fascinating. He would kill her. He *would*.

And yet he felt sick just thinking about it.

Meanwhile, Lady Beaumont stared out from the highest window of her estate on the fourth floor, black fabrics swirling around her, red fingernails tapping gently against the sides of her wine glass. She watched the town of Bellvoir move beneath her, and she imagined she could see the raven man himself, imagined the fear he felt knowing she was coming for him.

No, she would wait to see how things played out. The festival was tomorrow and then the ball the night after. Yes, that was when he would strike.

But she would be ready.

With the faintest smile, Eleanor Beaumont glided from her window and disappeared inside her expansive house, and as she did this, Regis walked the opposite way, thinking he ought to get himself a drink.

Sitting on a park bench watching him from across the street, a man with clown shoes and itchy makeup looked up from his newspaper. *He's the one they spoke of,* thought the clown, his eyes following the raven man until he was out of sight. *The tyrant in the gutter.*

If he murdered Lady Midnight, the rest of France would burn.

V

A NIGHT AT THE CABARET

eleste bought three dresses, then treated herself with an expensive pink hat, some jewellery and a black chatelaine purse, all before the clock tower chimed five o'clock in the evening.

After dropping everything back home, changing into a simple aquamarine dress, and setting her pink hat neatly on top of her made-up blonde hair, she visited a small restaurant down the road where she ate by herself. *Confit de canard,* a dish of duck that she had never been able to afford during the war. A band was up on stage playing soft but interesting folk music. The black man who was singing had a strong, bass voice and he occasionally smiled warmly at the passing waitresses and patrons.

A politician by the name of Gustave Mathieu was eating a dish of white bean cassoulet with his wife, his seven-year-old daughter and eighteen-year-old son. The family sat on a table by themselves and nobody bothered them, which Gustave liked very much. The polls hadn't been good to him lately and an election victory wasn't looking likely. The rest of the party wanted him to step down, citing their worst campaign in years. Gustave thought, maybe that would be a good idea. The way they spoke about him in the press—how they spoke about his family, too! The people of this town were cruel, borderline sinister.

"Gustave," his wife said.

He looked up, startled. His wife was staring at him very intently. She did not like how he looked these days, sunken eyes, ruffled hair and that terrible posture of his. She also did not approve of the way he made his son and daughter look at him—with concern. Everybody was concerned these days about Gustave. *He's always working,* the women whispered to her. He came home from the offices sometimes after midnight and then the papers in the morning talked about how he and his party were polling their lowest numbers since Antony stepped down in 1890. And then, of course, *she* would be drawn into it—and her children too.

Gustave's wife stared at Gustave for a long time but her husband's eyes were withdrawn. Their face-off was broken only by an arm, which belonged to Theo, their eldest, as he reached across the table to take the ketchup.

A few tables over, Celeste made accidental eye contact with the young man called Theo and immediately turned away, her cheeks burning. Theo wondered who that girl on the other table was. He remembered her from earlier that day when he'd given her that pamphlet. Judging by her meal and her presence here, she was wealthier than he'd thought.

Celeste played with her food, trying to hide the fact she'd been listening in on their conversation. A waiter came by her table and asked if she wanted anything else, but Celeste declined with a soft smile. She flipped open her pocket watch and saw that it was nearly six o'clock and she ought to be going back to the cabaret bar to watch Aurélie perform.

Feeling quite full, she stood up and vanished.

A tall man with a top hat stepped into the restaurant from the toilets out the back, his gloved hand leaving his coat pocket and plucking the cigar from his mouth, blowing smoke into the air.

Celeste spotted him just as she was about to leave but didn't think much of him, other than he was dressed for the wrong occasion. Gustave Mathieu saw him just as he finished the last sip of his drink, and his mouth went immediately dry.

The man waited by the toilets as people brushed past him, some of them complaining. He did not move, just stared at Gustave with those dark eyes.

"We should leave," Gustave said to his family.

Another man, on the other side of the restaurant, finished his last fork-full of pasta and reached for the orange-stained serviette to clean his mouth. This man's name was Ludovic and he worked for the press under a fake name. None could say which named Ludovic was. When he saw the man in the long coat come out of the toilet, the first thing he did was look around to see who else was in attendance tonight. There were few others of any significance. Just Gustave.

The family stood up together and began to leave.

Ludovic stood up and glanced back at the man in the coat. His name was Pascal and he worked for a man who worked for Ludovic. As Gustave and his family left, Ludovic drew a pistol and Pascal drew a pistol and they followed them.

A NIGHT AT THE CABARET

—◦—

THE RED WINDOWS OF THE BLACK DIME CABARET glowed at night. The walls seemed taller, stark black brick glossed with the moonlight and the red hue from the windows. Smoke curdled in the air from the cigars of wealthy, important men, and tickets were sold at a lit-up vendor just outside the entrance. A healthy line stood there.

Celeste walked straight in, shivering in the cold.

Aurélie took the stage at a quarter to eight to respectful applause and a few drunken jeers from the men. She was mid-thirties and very beautiful, dressed in red lace and red lipstick, with heels that lifted her from the ground. The band began to play.

"Here's your drink," Léa said as she returned to Celeste's table with two glasses: one of absinthe, one of wine. She was not wearing her masquerade mask, just pale makeup and glossed-up lips, her strawberry blonde hair perfectly loud. She took the wine and Celeste took the absinthe and they knocked their glasses together.

"Thank you," Celeste said.

"She is very good, isn't she?" Léa said.

Celeste nodded. "I'm impressed."

"Aurélie has been a member of the Black Dime

for as long as I can remember. We must have arrived within weeks of each other. I remember she was still very young when I got here. They love her now. I mean, would you look at them all?"

Aurélie sang the closing lyrics of a song, her sultry voice ringing out across the bar. She smiled, her red lips glistening under the glare of the stage lights. A curl of deep brown hair freed itself from her immaculate headdress and settled across her rosy cheeks as she bowed. The crowd erupted in applause.

Léa leaned across the table, gently knocking aside the candle and the rose that sat between them, and said, "The men come to proposition her. They think because we dress up and sing them songs that we're running some kind of brothel. They like to imagine the stories of what goes on here. Some of it's quite exciting, I won't lie. Unfortunately, it really is as simple as it looks." She paused, receding into the shadows as she took a sip of her wine, every blink revealing glittering eyelids. "Marguerite tells all sorts of stories to them."

"She's the woman at the bar," Celeste said.

"She runs the place, yes," Léa said with a sigh, gazing to the stage as the band launched into another song, bouncy and seductive. She was proud of Aurélie, for sure. The two of them had joined the Black Dime at a similar time, both of them very young. But everyone knew Aurélie now, even those who never attended a single show. She was nearly as famous as Eleanor herself, except Eleanor rarely made an appearance anywhere anymore.

Léa rested her wine on the table, catching a glimpse from Celeste as she did, and slotted a cigarette between her lips. "We could use someone like you here," she said, pulling out a match and striking it against the matchbox. A flame burst to life with a crack and fizzle. Celeste flinched, seeing the firelight reflected in Léa's amber eyes. "Fresh blood." She took a drag of the cigarette and exhaled a cool blossom of smoke, which sailed to the ceiling with style.

"Who was my great grandfather?" Celeste asked.

Léa sucked on the cigarette for a while, staining it red with lipstick. "Your great grandfather founded the Black Dime Cabaret in 1792. They called him the Count of Bellvoir," she said with theatre, "the most feared and ruthless yet revered man in all of France!" She laughed softly, then took another drag of the cigarette. Celeste watched her intently, painted by the violet lights emanating from the stage. "He was never married but the women loved him—and he loved them too, maybe. He was always good to the ladies and he was a good businessman on top of it. I suppose that's where it started." She tapped the table with her fingers. "This bar has been here for a century and now they want to tear it all down, and all for what? To build more houses over it, I guess."

"They're going to tear it down?" Celeste asked.

"We've lost every investor we have."

It seemed odd to Celeste. Look at the crowds, at the smiles on their drunken faces, their cheers and the talent of the Black Dime itself. "There's nothing else to do in Bellvoir!" she exclaimed.

"Exactly!" Léa said, waving smoke in the air.

"It sounds like a stupid idea."

"It's all just politics, isn't it?"

She studied Celeste now, as the song finished and the band gave bows to the sound of cheers and hollering. Celeste reminded her, not only of herself, but of Aurélie too. But there was Eleanor in her eyes. Not characteristically—hers were sky blue while Eleanor's were hauntingly green—but when Léa looked at Celeste she saw the same thing that she saw when she looked at Eleanor, and such a feeling was difficult to explain. So much so that she simply drew another tobacco-filled breath and ignored it.

All Bellvoir was nowadays was politics and Léa hated it.

"Did Count Lucien know he had a child?" Celeste asked.

"He killed himself before the child was born." She paused in contemplation, then said, "Nobody knew much about the Count. He lived a private life contrary to anything I may have said. He gave the spotlight to others."

A loud piano hit startled Celeste, temporarily disorienting her. The lights went red and Aurélie shed her overcoat to cheers from the crowd. Two performers joined their table, a man with white makeup and green pants, and a woman in a flowery black corset, a top hat and a painted moustache.

They were twins. The woman was three minutes older.

She tossed a pistol onto the table and plucked out a cigarette. A waitress glided by and the corset girl ordered more drinks for the table. The man in the white makeup slid the pistol over to himself and picked it up, pointing it at Celeste.

She started, gripping her dress fabrics underneath the table. She was staring directly into the barrel of the pistol, the smell of smoke and copper in her nose.

"They say it's a bad omen to die in a cabaret," the man said.

"People always die here, that's why they say business is booming," the girl said.

Léa choked on her smoke as she pointed to the newcomers. "That's Vincent and Jacqueline, and no that pistol isn't real otherwise I would have chopped off Vincent's hand."

Vincent pulled the trigger and pink glitter exploded from the barrel. Celeste flinched, finding that her palms had become quite sweaty. Vincent spun the pistol around his finger, guiding it through a loop-de-loop. Celeste watched it intently.

"I'm Celeste," she said through the cloud of glitter and smoke.

She felt the ground rumble underneath her feet and she gripped the table in an effort to steady herself. The candle upon the tabletop flickered softly as the crash of a drum blasted through the bar, prickling the hairs on her arms.

She was no longer in the cabaret but in a tavern in Northern France. Sitting opposite her was a young blue-eyed soldier with a shocking beard and tussled hair, an eyepatch covering his left eye and his bandaged-up hand raising a drink to his cracked lips. The ground rumbled. The walls shook. They always did, the earth moving and shifting under Celeste's feet. She was only a day after eighteen but she felt like she'd been on the battlefield for thirty years.

"How do you like the music?" the man said.

There was music? Yes, a small band in the corner, brass and drums and a baritone voice. Celeste looked around. How had she ended up here? The tavern was small and insignificant, dead animals hanging from the walls, lanterns separating them. Other soldiers walked around with muskets slung across their shoulders and large jugs of beer sloshing between them.

"I like it," Celeste said carefully.

"The drink?" the man said.

Drink? It was on the table in front of her, a light froth sitting on top. She took it and downed the rest of it, banging it onto the table.

"Not many women on the battlefield," the man said.

Celeste regarded him warily. *I don't think I should be here,* she thought, thinking of the music and the soldiers and the drinks. *I think I'm in the wrong place.*

"I have to go," she said. She grabbed her nurse's hat and stood up from the table, balancing it back on her blonde hair. She glanced at the door. Another soldier stood there, smoking a cigarette and nursing a bandaged head wound.

"Why so soon?" Somebody grabbed her from

behind and slammed her against the wall. She yelped but his mouth was on hers and then someone yelled to buy a room at the inn next door and she could smell blood and alcohol and cigarettes and he tore her dress and—

Aurélie was singing again and the lights had dimmed.

She was staring at the man with the pale makeup but she knew in that moment she had never seen him before. He was just another member of the Black Dime. Léa was looking at Celeste, sensing a disturbance. She did not look particularly well, gone suddenly pale. Léa noticed how she had gripped the edge of the table, how her bottom lip quivered.

"Simonne wants to put on a contemporary rendition of *The Bride of Messina*," Jacqueline was saying in a bitter voice. "But I keep telling her, there's no way Marguerite will approve of that—and Marguerite approves of nearly anything."

"How about you, Celeste?" Vincent said. "Do you watch much theatre?"

Léa studied how Celeste responded to the question. She seemed startled at first, as if she'd forgotten Vincent was even there. She then shrugged, picking up her glass of absinthe and taking the smallest sip. "A little bit," was all she said.

Celeste was thinking about the war again and how she'd never really had much of a chance to go to the theatre. She'd been too poor to see it growing up, and she had never caught much of a break on the battlefield. Except for that one time.

"There was one show," she remembered. "Offenbach's *La Périchole*. I don't think I've heard anything more beautiful in my life." And that was the truth. She could even hear it now. The crescendo of strings and the thunderous timpani and soaring French horns. The majestic Anna Judic, who had stepped out to embody the titular role for the very last time, her voice like no voice Celeste had ever heard. She sometimes wondered if she had heard it at all, or if that had all just been some fever dream.

"*La Périchole* is one of my favourites," Léa said.

"I might go to the bathroom," Celeste said as she stood up from her chair and the crowd broke into applause for Aurélie. Her head was throbbing and each step she took caused the room to tilt, the alcohol knocking the walls of her stomach.

She was halfway across the cabaret when she saw that politician again, Gustave, from the restaurant, except this time without his family. He wore the same suit but was drinking with a woman who was not his wife. She was beautiful, rosy cheeked and with gorgeous blonde hair and a scandalous red dress. Celeste paused, watching the two of them.

Gustave got up and kissed the woman, and then left the building. Celeste watched him until he was gone, the woman brushing down her dress and wiping her lips with disgust. In her hands was a cheque book and a slip of paper. An elderly couple brushed past Celeste, throwing her closer to where the woman was standing, glancing around suspiciously. Her eyes met Celeste's for a heartbeat and Celeste withdrew.

The woman wondered who that was, finding something . . . familiar about the way she looked and then so nervously glanced away. It didn't matter, she deduced, folding away the slip of paper and the chequebook, having just collected a rather large sum from Gustave Mathieu. What a sad, pathetic waste of a man. So easily manipulated. No wonder the people hated him. Soon, she supposed, when there was nobody left to hate, they might turn their eyes towards other targets. The woman suspected there would be chaos.

Chaos suited the Black Dime.

When Celeste looked again, the woman was gone.

Gustave left the cabaret and walked through an alleyway back home in the middle of the night. Yellow lamps lit the cobbled path ahead, and he followed them, dodging scurrying rats and beggars along the sidewalks, who huddled under the eaves of tenements.

He tucked in his shirt and fixed his hair. He still reeked of the woman but there was nothing he could do about that besides take the long way home and hope the Bellvoir air cleansed him of it. As he thought about her now, Charlotte, he felt a pang of depression set in. How different things might have been had he never gotten married, never thought that settling down would somehow bring him happiness when he had never been happy his whole life. He felt like a rat that had become infected with the plague, doomed to suffer until death came, and to death he'd walk with open arms.

He lit a cigarette and stopped at the mouth of the alleyway, gazing out upon a crossroads which was empty save for a few council workers. One of them whistled softly as he climbed a ladder to a lamp and hung things there. Another walked along the road with his broom, sweeping leaves from the gutters.

How miserable, Gustave thought as he strolled into the crossroads. One man who was rolling a barrel along the ground looked up but he was too far to make out anything discerning. Gustave nibbled on the end of his cigarette, then spat smoke into the cold air.

"What's with all the bloody rats in this town!" Gustave shrieked.

A few others perked up at this and one responded, "Sod off, you bastard."

"They keep telling me there's a plague but then why aren't any of us fucking dead!" He laughed, flicking the cigarette onto the cobbles and crushing it with his foot. Wisps of smoke sprang up into his face and he waved them away tiredly.

"There's no plague," the guy rolling the barrel said, reaching a spot along the storefronts and hauling up the barrel so that it was standing upright. "You live in the gutter, you get sick. Rats carry disease but a plague that can wipe out France? Nah, man."

"How do you buy yourself a vote around here?" Gustave said, stepping on a rat's tail. It squeaked, its tail straining under his foot. He stared down at it, watching how pathetic it looked. At last, he let it go and the rat fled.

"Wait..." A man jumped down from his ladder and slowly walked up to Gustave, shining a lantern at his face. Gustave squinted, shielding his eyes. "You're the politician."

Gustave cleared his throat, suddenly feeling exposed.

"Well that does explain many things!" the man

said, spitting at him. Gustave flinched, the glob of spittle barely missing his pants. "Piss off then!"

"I'm sorry," Gustave muttered under his breath.

"Oi!" that same man yelled. "This is that bastard who fucked us in the arse!"

A few other workers came with their various building tools, their shadows long and uneven across the cobbled road. Gustave tried to back off and nearly lost his footing.

One of the men snarled at him. "One of these days you'll get what you deserve."

"Would you please get out of my face," Gustave said with a tremor.

The man spat on him. "I hope you rot. I hope your whore wife rots. I hope your children die by the rats. You're sick and twisted, all you politicians. I hope you all fucking—"

A gunshot rang out and blood splashed across Gustave, hitting him square in the face. The worker went down. Lanterns went up. Two figures stepped out of the shadows, pistols blowing smoke in the wind, and set the crossroads alight with muzzle flashes. Bodies thudded to the cobblestones in sloppy puddles of blood. Gustave screamed, covering his ears as he stood over their dead bodies. Blood dribbled down his face. Cowering and shaking, he half-raised his hands and turned to the sound of a pistol being reloaded.

"Help me!" Gustave screamed.

Another gunshot rang out and Gustave went flying, pain scorching his gut. He landed several feet away on his back, grabbing his stomach. Blood squirted between his fingers in a pumping rhythm, drenching his crumpled white suit.

The two phantoms approached him.

The smaller of the two extended his arm and pointed the pistol at Gustave's face. Gustave looked at it, tears carving trails through the other man's blood. "Wait . . ." he sobbed. "I don't know what I've done but please have mercy. I was a fool." He screeched, a sudden burst of pain squelching through him. "Please . . ."

"Your first mistake was crossing paths with Mister Archambault," said the man with the gun as his companion raised his firing arm, too. "Your final mistake was double-crossing him."

"I'm sorry, sir," Gustave whimpered.

Gunshots rang out in the cold, dark night of Bellvoir. Rats darted from the violent splashes of muzzle fire. A cat screamed, its tail going taut before it sprinted out of sight. Gustave's dead body hit the ground with such force his skull cracked, bullets pinning him like nails. The two suited men drew a harmonious sigh and holstered their pistols. A light went on in one of the nearby tenements and a curtain was drawn to the side, but by the time the young wife had rubbed her eyes clear of sleep, the two men were gone and only bodies remained.

From a dark office building in another district, Mister Archambault sat on his chair with his legs kicked up on the table. Moonlight reflected off his spectacles. A wall clock slowly ticked and Mister Archambault's fingers drummed the newspaper on his lap.

It would begin making the rounds first thing tomorrow morning.

The headline: WITCHES MASSACRE GUSTAVE MATHIEU.

VI

WITCHES IN BELLVOIR

erdinand sat in the backseat of a *Panhard* automobile, letting the rumble of the engine calm his nerves. Laurent occupied the seat beside him, slowly flicking through the morning newspaper.

"There's something severely wrong with this city, Laurent," Ferdinand said, watching the passing scenery. It was the early morning and workers were finalising preparations for the parade. "Corruption. Greed. Rats carrying plague. There's no respite. Not in the coldest, quietest corner. Not anywhere." He tore his gaze from the streets to Laurent, his face as passive and unassuming as ever. "Witches, Laurent! I told you!"

Laurent said nothing, turning another page. The top story, and this story was all over the papers, churned out in record time, was that witches had murdered Gustave Mathieu last night. There were also others but Gustave was the politician, which made it political. There was, of course, no evidence of witches—the men had been shot to death—but whatever the papers said became the truth, so it was witches after all. But when they said "witches" they really meant Lady Beaumont. Laurent didn't know who killed Mister Mathieu but he was keeping an open mind. Headlines had no business telling the truth. Mister Archambault, who owned a fair stake in the papers, had been a propaganda minister in the war.

"Won't you say something?" Ferdinand grumbled.

"It *is* awkward," Laurent said as he folded up the paper. "Witches murdering innocent people on the streets. The headlines are telling us to burn them at the stake, the day is telling us, well,"—he flipped open his little pocket diary—"ah, yes, to celebrate them."

"Aren't you just the slightest bit concerned, Laurent?"

Laurent shrugged. In all honesty, he did not feel too concerned at all. He smiled softly, propping up his glasses and putting on his kindest voice, his reassuring voice. "May I ask what your exact concern is?"

Ferdinand groaned and yanked the newspaper from Laurent's grasp, unfolding it so that he could perfectly read the front page headline. "Witches killed Gustave Mathieu last night, Laurent, and here we are riding to visit the woman who very well could have orchestrated it!"

"Oh, Lady Beaumont didn't kill Mister Mathieu," Laurent said.

"What are you talking about? Of course she did!"

"Very well, then she has just committed electoral suicide."

Ferdinand scoffed, utterly bewildered. "What?"

"You can't expect to win an election by going out and murdering everybody, you do realise? Even if you were successful, becoming elected simply because you were the last candidate standing, the French people would rebel. We have just come out of another war, Ferdinand. Those tactics don't work anymore, and Lady Beaumont more than anybody can't be trying those tactics simply because of what the people think she is. She has nothing to gain. However . . ." He slowed down, glancing outside as they passed two policemen tending a flower vendor. "It does make our alliance seem a lot more beneficial."

"Hm," Ferdinand said, scratching at his beard.

"We provide funding for her cabaret operation, as well as our protection—which, given the times, could prove invaluable. I pull some strings in the press and we take some of the heat off her, get rid of those incriminating headlines. An imbecile would know that Lady Beaumont's election chances are all but obliterated as of right now."

"Then who killed Gustave?"

Laurent took a second to think about this. "We don't know, and we don't have to know."

"Ok, so what if Lady Beaumont *did* kill him?" Even as he said it, Ferdinand realised there was a large part of him that was trying to build the scenario of her killing him, that it was true and there *were* in fact witches in Bellvoir, because that would just make things so much easier. After all, the alternative was that someone was killing people and it could be anyone, and Ferdinand had pissed off his fair share of Frenchmen in this town.

"If Lady Beaumont is out here murdering her

competition," Laurent said drily, turning his head to meet Ferdinand's eyes, "then I suppose we ought to cancel that lunch this evening."

———

THE AUTOMOBILE PULLED UP OUTSIDE LADY Beaumont's house and two pairs of shoes stepped out. The first were rather nice shoes, perhaps overly expensive, and brown dress pants that had been tailored perhaps too many times and too much, pinching a rather fat physique. The second were still nice shoes, brand name, but not French—the owner of these shoes clearly valued more oriental design and had paid a premium to import them. His pants were stone blue and a perfect fit, and it was clear that this man knew fashion far more than his companion.

Ferdinand shivered as he walked from the black car and stared up the stone stairs to the chilling façade of Eleanor Beaumont's manor house. Skeletal autumn trees painted a horrifying picture. There was no sign of life save for a ghoulish-looking man along the walkway raking orange leaves from the footpath, back into the gardens.

Laurent followed him up the winding footpath, tasting a staleness in the air. The winds moved slower here, the only sound their footsteps on the uneven path. The groundskeeper stopped raking the leaves and watched them approach, no expression on his pinched face. Ferdinand glanced at him once but averted his eyes, feeling a chill drip through his spine. Laurent gave the man a polite nod and the man did not respond, eyeing him with suspicion.

A very timely visit, the ghoulish man thought.

Ferdinand and Laurent reached the front door and rang the bell. They waited. Ferdinand patted down his white shirt and red overcoat, feeling knots of tension gripping various parts of his body. *This is a dreadful idea,* he thought. He became suddenly aware of his life up until this moment, and his accomplishments—of which there were very little. What a terrible way to die, to have it all end because you willingly walked into a witch's house the morning after she openly murdered seven people including an election candidate.

Laurent rang the bell again and waited.

I shouldn't have brought Ferdinand, he thought.

The doors creaked open and a face poked through. Laurent's heart skipped a beat for the first time in many years. The face through the parting in the door was the very same one outside raking the leaves. Ferdinand gasped and went pale but Laurent simply stood there as the butler smiled.

"Lady Beaumont will see you upstairs," he said kindly. Laurent thanked him and stepped inside. He felt an immediate lack of emotion, seeing everything as objectively as possible. The walls and the paintings, the carpeted floors and the stairwell that extended upwards into the manor house heights.

Another butler revealed himself from the shadows, identical to the two before him. He wore a black suit and a white cravat. "If you would follow me, gentlemen."

They followed him up the stairs.

"Lady Beaumont has been anticipating your arrival," the butler said, not looking at them. "It was a welcome surprise. The Lady does not always take kindly to invitations."

"We are grateful," Laurent said as firmly as he could.

At the fourth floor landing, the butler stopped by a single mahogany door and gently pushed it open for them. Laurent and Ferdinand walked into the chamber of Eleanor Beaumont. The vaulted ceiling carved an invisible path directly towards arched floor-to-ceiling windows, all with a striking red tint. The architecture was classical and woody.

Laurent noted the way Ferdinand stayed a few paces behind him, and once they stepped into the chamber, the opposition leader cautiously glanced over his shoulder as the butler closed the door. Laurent felt his mind uncloud the slightest bit, enough that he could now judge the eerie silence. *It's odd to be sure,* he thought. *What I saw out there is impossible.*

Lady Beaumont entered from a side room dressed in a long black gown. She stopped, judging them from afar, her gloved hands clasped. Her auburn hair burned underneath the red autumn light. "It is a pleasure," she said at last in a deceptively gentle voice. Laurent sensed her dishonesty. Lady Beaumont gestured to a couple of red couches on the edge of the room. "Tea?"

"Tea will be nice," Laurent answered.

He noted the way Lady Beaumont's emerald eyes turned ever-so-fleetingly to Ferdinand and he noticed a turn of the lip, but that was all. With the softest smile of tight red lips, she called for one of the butlers to come with tea. The three of them were seated on the couches, Lady Beaumont on one, Laurent and Ferdinand on another, steaming teacups in hand. The butler, who wore the very same face as all those before him, vanished out the large door.

Laurent took an immediate sip of the tea. It burned his tongue. The tea went down well. After a moment's thought, he determined the tea was not in fact poisoned.

"I don't receive many visitors," Lady Beaumont said.

"Eleanor Beaumont is not a socialite?" Laurent said, hinting at the fact it was widely reported that she was, or at least *had* been at some unknown point in history, possibly the greatest socialite who ever came to France.

"She is not anymore," Lady Beaumont said. "Laurent, was it? And Ferdinand Rousseau. I admire the work you have done in your campaign thus far. Please, call me Eleanor. I find the formalities begin to irk me at a point."

Ferdinand loudly slurped his tea and then said, his beard wet, "You may be the one woman in France who admires our work. The polls are, quite honestly, appalling."

"Christophe Archambault dictates the polls," Eleanor said.

"Biggest bastard in France," Ferdinand said.

"Hm. Well, I assume you've seen the headlines. I am surprised anybody would want to see me at all, knowing what they say about me. The lies they spread." She lifted the teacup to her lips, letting steam coalesce before her emerald eyes. She softly blew the surface of the tea, causing it to ripple. "To use such a tragedy to push a false agenda, all for votes . . ." She took a sip and the room became quiet except for the ticking of a clock, somewhere distant.

"If we believed those rumours," Laurent said, "we wouldn't be here. Christophe Archambault owns a large enough stake in those papers that anything you read during election times is prone to be propaganda. The man was raised on a steady diet of lies and cheating. It is oftentimes said that his own mother fooled him into thinking their family owned France itself."

Eleanor shrugged, indifferent. "Perhaps they did."

"Well she was a whore and her husband was a street rat."

"A whore or a street rat have never done anything worthwhile?"

Laurent swallowed, unbalanced. "If I have offended you, I apologise. I don't often spurt my mouth like that. Was simply venting my disappointment in the man."

"It is okay," Eleanor said with a smile, her cheeks rosy. "So tell me,"—she straightened her posture into one that resembled less a person and more the subject of a beautiful painting—"what is it that you wish to discuss?"

Laurent straightened and rested his cup of tea in his lap, careful not to burn through his expensive imported pants. "We were hoping, if this is something you would consider, to form somewhat of a political alliance that would benefit us both in various ways."

Eleanor seemed to consider this.

"We provide funding for your Black Dime Cabaret, and offer our protection, which includes physical threats and immunity against the defamation in the papers. Quell any talk of witches in Bellvoir, and the supposed violence they're causing. In exchange, we ask for only one thing: your endorsement in the election."

"You wish for me to drop out."

"Yes."

Eleanor stared at him, her face impossible to read.

"You will never be bothered again. Not you. Not the cabaret. There are other ways to undo injustices in this town. Other ways to make money."

"And you're my answer to that."

"I am offering one million francs. That's a promise."

Ferdinand choked on his tea but Eleanor Beaumont continued to eye him intently. "One million francs sounds like more than even a man of your calibre could have."

Laurent shrugged. "A man of my calibre has ways of acquiring such wealth."

"Why run for mayor?"

"Mister Rousseau is not after money."

"I see," Eleanor said, her voice monotone. "I suppose it would be unwise to deny the burgeoning crisis in Bellvoir. This city is cruel. The people are worse than rats. They leech everything from you until all you have left is the emptiness of an overlarge manor house. They make up lies to ruin your reputation, and then drink with you when you conquer them. Perhaps it is wishful thinking to believe the town won't turn against me."

She stood and offered her hand. Laurent climbed to his feet and took it. Eleanor held him, closing the distance between them, her black dress rolling along the carpet. "I accept your proposal. I will inform my party members to contact you personally with the terms." She turned from Laurent to Ferdinand and shook his hand, too. "I anticipate you to be men of your word."

"It has been a pleasure," Laurent said without answering.

"Thank you for coming to meet me," Eleanor said.

Laurent and Ferdinand walked side-by-side down the pathway back to their awaiting vehicle, the driver of it sitting on the bonnet smoking a cigarette, top hat on his head.

"Did you say *one million* francs?" Ferdinand whimpered.

"She was very receptive, wasn't she?" Laurent said.

"You don't have one million francs!"

"Whoops," Laurent said with a smile on his face.

"Gentlemen," the driver said as he slid from the bonnet and opened the *Panhard* doors for them. Laurent climbed in on one side, Ferdinand on the other.

"Bloody . . ." Ferdinand began. "Did you see the servants?"

"Yes," Laurent said, thinking of their identical faces. The white shirts and black waistcoats and the slight combovers. That placid expression, as if disconnected from the world.

"Odd?" Ferdinand said.

"I can confirm that, yes, that was odd."

The black doors closed and they drove from the house of Eleanor Beaumont without looking back. From the fourth floor window, Eleanor watched them until they were gone.

A ROTTING HAND SPLASHED TO THE COBBLED ground, the scream of its owner drowned out by the explosion of fireworks. And there were drums as the man yowled, his naked body swollen with black blisters and rot. A doctor in a mask fed him something sour and gross-tasting, making him gag until he eventually vomited it all out, bloody and grey. Trumpets sounded. The two doctors looked at each other. One pulled out a pistol. The naked man screamed and flew from their grasp as the town erupted in music and the doctor shot him in the back of the head.

A flock of birds darted from one of the skeleton trees, sending leaves drifting down to the streets of Bellvoir. A nest of rats crawled out of the gutter and dodged the falling leaves, scurrying to the street where the parade marched. One passed underneath a wooden seat, causing an old woman to shriek in disgust and jump to her feet.

A group of young boys, probably no older than twelve, snatched one of the rats and tortured it over a firepit, slashing off its tail with a knife stolen from one of their parents. One of the other rats saw this and fled from the scene.

Celeste followed Léa through a crowd of people

just as the procession filed past them, the sound of trumpets and percussion and zestful strings going off all around it. They broke out of the throng and the parade floated past them. Large depictions of witches sailed through the sky and people danced in witch clothing and makeup. A young man in a white suit, holding a prop of a nasty-looking witch, smiled at her and then was gone.

Celeste bumped into Léa, who had suddenly stopped.

It was morning when they spoke for the first time that day.

"I want you to meet Maria," Léa had told her, right about the time the newspapers had started circulating and news of witches in Bellvoir murdering election candidates had begun to spread like flames. They had been inside one of the guestrooms in Celeste's new house, where she had arranged her clothes. Léa was picking something out for her to wear. Not too dark. Not too gaudy. A celebratory autumn feel.

"Who's Maria?" Celeste asked as she tried on an orange hat.

Léa appeared behind her in the mirror's view and swept a large black dress in front of her, putting on a thoughtful expression. "Maria is the oldest woman in Bellvoir, unless there's another woman in

Bellvoir who is one hundred and twenty-nine years old."

"That's impossible," Celeste had said.

"Maria knew your great grandfather personally."

"You only told her now that I'm here?"

"No, she knew you were here," Léa said, spinning Celeste and pinching the black dress around her so tight she gasped. "It was just a matter of was she ready to revisit those memories—and to face the only known blood of Lucien himself."

And Celeste recalled this now as she stood amidst the crowd, trying to figure out who exactly Léa was looking for. *Maria knew Count Lucien, my great grandfather.*

"This way!" Léa said, leading Celeste through the crowds alongside the procession. She spotted Jacqueline from the night before, wearing a violet dress and gloves as she stood under a lamppost completely encircled with streamers.

"Did you see the papers?" Jacqueline said conspiratorially. Léa nodded. Jacqueline looked between her and Celeste. "Bastards! Well come on then."

The three women moved swiftly down the street, but their brief interaction had not gone unnoticed. Standing on the other side of the road, not taking part in the festivities and dressed in black like a man in mourning was young Theodore Mathieu, eldest son of Gustave. He had wanted to stay home, away from the sick festivities, with his mother and sister—but he couldn't bear it. Their cries. The constant whimpering, each moment reminding him of his dead father— murdered by witches, and here they were all over the city, a constant reminder.

There was something about those three women.

Concealing a pistol in his coat, he crossed the street and followed them. Celeste took no notice of the man behind them but Léa did, and she knew that he was the son of the murdered candidate, yet she ignored him. He would be a fool to follow them to Maria.

"Marguerite says everything proceeds as planned," Jacqueline said in her fast, clipped voice. "Eleanor is unhappy but she hopes to amend the situation sooner rather than later."

"She didn't kill those people, did she?" Léa said quietly.

"They were shot to death," Jacqueline said. "Of course not."

Celeste followed them from the parade to a small neighbourhood near the house of Eleanor Beaumont, near enough that when the sun slipped towards the horizon, the shadow cast from Lady Beaumont's manor house covered this smaller one. A boy carrying newspapers on a bike struck his bell as he clumsily skirted them. A belated "sorry" rang out as he disappeared in the distance. Red leaves flipped up from the gravel and Celeste brushed one as it landed against her onyx dress.

She looked up at the house. Mason jars hung from the eaves, clattering melodically in the breeze. There was an immediate smell of plants and vegetables. She saw strawberries and mushrooms growing in pots against the windows. The wooden façade was painted a dull white, and the wood was splintered in places, rotting away. Where the roof became a steeple, she noticed a round window blocked out by pink curtains. Except a black cat's head poked out from between the part in the curtains, and it watched her.

I do not like her, the cat thought. Behind the cat was a slow draught of heavy breathing, and the bed creaked and groaned as Maria, the cat's owner, lay there half awake.

Celeste shivered as she ignored the cat and climbed the stairs to the front door. Jacqueline knocked three times. The door opened and a dwarf was staring up at them. He did not look in any way pleased to see them, his face pinched and his eyes suspicious, as he glared out from behind the metal security door.

"You've brought the girl?" he said, looking at Celeste. "I see." The door squealed open and the dwarf invited them inside. He continued to watch this new arrival as she walked past him into the dark living room. Then, scratching at his orange and yellow striped sweater, he shut the door and followed them inside. "I'm André. A pleasure to meet you."

"I'm Celeste," Celeste responded.

"Maria hasn't been well. She's sleeping upstairs."

Celeste watched him walk into the kitchen and prepare the kettle. The house was nice. The living room consisted of a greyish green rug and a wooden table, and in the corner was a rocking chair draped with a blue woollen blanket. There were old paintings on the walls, many of them discoloured and frayed. Celeste walked from the group, examining them. A young woman, perhaps twenty, posed in front of a garden of roses. There was a man in a commander's uniform adorned with badges, with an incredibly good yellow moustache.

"That's her," Léa said, pointing at the portrait of the young woman. She was quite pretty, blonde hair made up in tumbling locks, her expression placid yet

112

sweet, her skin ghost-like in the faded colours of old paint.

"And who's the man?" Celeste asked.

"That's her father. Alfred Lucien. The younger brother to your great grandfather. The two men bore a striking resemblance but for a few key features, particularly the moustache."

Celeste frowned. "Maria is one of my great grandfather's cousins?"

"His youngest cousin and the last surviving member of the Lucien bloodline, until you came along. She doesn't talk to many people and her memory isn't as it always was, but I hope she'll be able to understand who you are. And if not, well, it would be difficult to blame her."

André hobbled up to them. "Shall we head upstairs?"

"Sure," Celeste said with a nod.

The dwarf thought for a moment, glancing between the three women—Jacqueline was sitting on a couch in the living room, staring outside the window. "Perhaps it would be best," André said, "if only the girl came to see her. Maria doesn't like too many guests."

Celeste looked to Léa for affirmation, and she nodded.

André nodded sternly and then turned and led the way.

THEODORE STOOD IN FRONT OF THE HOUSE WHERE the women went, the feel of his pistol still thrumming against his palm despite the fact he'd concealed it again. He needed answers. He needed to see justice be served against those witches.

Were they witches? Were the headlines true?

"Meow," said a cat.

Theodore jumped. A black cat with gleaming emerald eyes leapt up onto a nearby trash bin and stared at him, purring softly. This cat had a new name, Nette, and she thought it a fitting one. "Shoo!" Theodore said to the cat.

Don't go in there, thought the cat, and Theodore heard it resounding through his own mind. He had now completely forgotten the feel of the pistol in his hands. All he knew now was the cat.

Nette approached him, standing on the edge of the bin.

"What are you?" Theodore croaked.

Run away from this place, Nette howled into his mind.

Theodore did not need to be told twice. Feeling a sudden rush of horror, he did exactly as the cat instructed, running away from that place and not looking back.

THERE WAS ANOTHER BLACK CAT, THIS ONE ON the top floor of Maria's house. She made brief eye contact with the cat below and then turned from the pink curtains, stalking through the cold room. She stopped by the old standing mirror, which was covered in a layer of dust, lifting her leg and licking her fur clean. A groan came from the stairs and the cat paused with her tongue still hanging out of her mouth. She glanced across the dark attic to the bed with its woollen blankets. Maria was awake. The cat prowled into a small spot of light as André appeared with a girl in his wake.

"Clotilde, leave us," André said.

The cat meowed at him and darted down the stairs.

"Who goes there?" Maria croaked, sitting up. The bedframe creaked when she moved. Her voice was weak and barely carried across the room. "André?"

"Yes, Maria, it's André." He crossed the room to the bed. Celeste approached with caution. The first thing she noticed was the off smell, a combination of urine and mould. Maria was a sickly sight, shrivelled up like a century-old prune, her eyes sewn shut by detritus and filth. Her wrinkles were so deep they cast their own shadows from the candle beside her bed.

"There is someone else," Maria whispered.

"I've brought someone who would like to meet you," André said as he pulled out a wooden chair and beckoned for Celeste to sit down. Slowly, she entered the very small ambit lit by Maria's candle and felt the air become significantly colder.

A spider who was sitting on a broken table clock hissed as André came over and swatted it with a brush, shattering its web and dispersing its babies. André stared down at the spider in disgust before motioning for it to leave. The spider obeyed, racing along the wooden dressing table and through a crack in the wall.

Maria's heavy, uneven breathing filled the room.

The floorboards creaked as André returned, standing at Maria's bedside and resting a hand on her thin shoulder. There wasn't much of her, just bone and sinew. Her off-white nightgown patterned with yellow ducklings drooped off her shoulder for it had become two sizes too large. The ducklings frowned, creases forming in their depressed, discoloured faces.

"Maria, this is Celeste," André said.

Maria said nothing, just turned her head. Her eyelids quivered but they did not open. "Who is she, dear?"

"Celeste. Celeste *Lucien*, Maria."

Maria shivered, her skeletal hand gripping the bedsheets.

Celeste felt her own hand closing the space between them, like in the medical tents on the battlefield. "I think you knew my great grandfather," she said, gently touching Maria's hand.

Maria jerked away with ferocity. "Get her away from me!" she yowled, yanking up the bedsheets as a shield. André began stroking her silver hair. *"Make her leave!"*

"It's okay, Maria. She's a Lucien . . . like you."

"Should I leave?" Celeste said. She glanced at André and he looked back at her, but said nothing, just gave the impression that she should stay. He cradled Maria as though she were his baby, caressed her straw-like hair until she calmed down, spittle hanging from her lip.

"Lucien . . ." Maria whispered through chattering teeth.

André lifted the bedsheets to Maria's lips and wiped the drool from them. "Yes, Maria. This is

Celeste Lucien. She would just like to talk. Is that okay?"

"André, I'm scared," Maria said.

He held her tight and told her there was nothing to be scared of, but he also looked at Celeste and wondered what Maria could see. He trusted the witches of the Black Dime enough to believe Celeste was who they said she was, but he also knew that Maria was the wisest of them all, and she had not become this frightened in a long time.

In fact, not since ...

A figure appeared in his mind's eye with the sound of lightning, but the lightning was red, and then it became flames, and he heard screams and the wailing of children.

Maria had not shown this sort of fear since Seraphine, the witch of Carcassonne.

But she was calm now. He had her hand in his— he held her lightly, careful so as not to cause her any harm.

"Celeste ..." Maria breathed. "Celeste ..."

Celeste leaned forward but only the slightest bit. She had never seen somebody so frail in her entire life. Not the wounded on the battlefields of France. Not the mangled corpses who lined the trenches. Not the poor folk in the border towns. She felt a sadness envelop her as she took in the sight of the old woman, somebody waiting to die. "Can you tell me more about my family?" Celeste asked very quietly.

Maria stared at her with her cracked lips apart. The room became so quiet Celeste could hear the traffic outside, the whistling of the wind as it sailed through the trees, the musical chattering of the mason jars hanging from the eaves outside.

"Take your time," André said to her.

"What else is there to say?" Maria said. "Edgar Lucien was a good man."

Celeste smiled. "What was he like? Did you know his son? Or his daughter?"

Maria thought, smiling for the very first time. When she smiled, her cracked lips split and a small pool of blood began to form, which André hastily wiped. "He always very much wanted a son or a daughter. It was his last wish before he passed. And ... I've always thought it a horrible shame that he never got to know her name."

"Antoinette?" Celeste asked.

Maria nodded but with sadness.

"Who was the mother?"

At this, Maria truly took pause. Celeste noted the way her eyelids quivered and her wrinkles shook, lips parted as if to speak but only letting out a soft wheeze. "She . . ."

Fire burned from a letter dated 1815 and a woman walked away from it with stolen jewels on her fingers. Three months later, in the bathroom of an expensive manor house, she discovered she was pregnant. Everything happened very fast. When the child was born, the woman was weak from carrying him, and she was only young herself.

"Take her from me," were her last known words.

Maria searched the young woman's green eyes. A gust of wind and ice blew through the alleyway by the train station, causing Maria to cling to her winter's cowl. Snow pelted the cobbled road. A flame was snuffed out.

The child, wrapped up in blankets, wriggled in Maria's arms.

"You would not abandon your child," Maria said, dismayed.

The woman just stared back at her, moonlight catching her green irises. Like emeralds, as bright as anything Maria had ever seen, and yet a soul so dark . . .

The woman turned and fled for the train station.

"Rosalie!" Maria screamed. "Stop!"

Celeste saw the scene in her mind's eye. She felt

a tear roll down her face. One rolled down Maria's, becoming trapped in her cheeks.

"I never saw that woman again," Maria said softly.

"They were not married, were they," Celeste said.

Maria shook her head. "She was no Lucien. My dear . . ." She reached out her hand and Celeste took it this time, carefully. Maria pulled her closer until they were so close Celeste could feel the weight of every breath she took, each one a miracle. "There is a book." She pointed with a trembling finger across the room to a wooden chest. "It is yours."

"Thank you for telling me that," Celeste said.

Maria opened her hand to reveal a small, golden key. "Now please . . . let me sleep."

Celeste took the key, rose from the chair and walked to the wooden chest. The cat Clotilde watched her from the staircase, her tail low and her ears peeled back. The girl was unfamiliar but she gave off a horrid aura. The air seemed to grow still wherever she walked. But Celeste was unaware of this, kneeling by the chest and identifying the lock.

Her hand trembled with anticipation as she inserted the golden key into the lock and turned it. With a click, the chest opened.

A large leatherbound book lay inside it.

The Principles of Witchcraft, Volume I.

The author: Edgar Lucien.

"There were only two copies of that," Maria said from the bed, her voice filled with more ferocity than before. Celeste lifted the book from the chest and stared at Maria across the room. The woman's eyes were wide now, revealing white eyeballs, only one of which still contained a pupil—but the pupil was dislodged, halfway in the back of her head, occasionally twitching.

"Where's the other one?" Celeste asked.

"The other one boarded a train seventy-eight years ago with Rosalie Beaumont."

VII

GRAVEYARD GATHERING

magician with a purple hat and a green suit sang a magic word, waved his wand and then tossed it upwards majestically as fireworks exploded overhead, illuminating the crepuscular evening sky. The children who gathered around him yelped and cheered, their frayed and dirty shoes thumping against the cobbled road.

A shooting star split the clouds, leaving behind a wound of red light, which slowly bled and dribbled crimson across the highest buildings of Bellvoir. On the balcony of one of those buildings stood Eleanor Beaumont, the silvery hem of her black dress grabbing her ankles and undulating in the soft evening breeze. She stood by the railing overlooking the town, watching the fireworks and listening to the music from a folk band nearby.

Bellvoir was beautiful at night, and she meant that with her heart. Once, she had walked those streets with the people, had sung songs in the Black Dime Cabaret, danced and laughed and drank good wine. She sometimes wondered how she'd become so jaded. Time? All this time spent alone in her manor house, perhaps? Would she dare show her face, even if she could? Did the people not despise her? Make up false rumours of her killing campaigners?

Running for mayor of Bellvoir was her idea. It was her way of righting the injustices that were happening every day across those streets she so often gazed upon. Save the Black Dime Cabaret. There was a plague in France, a terrible plague, killing hundreds every day. She would not stand by and watch them be doused in fire. Watch them rot. And yet they said the plague was her doing. What mattered? The truth or what they believed? They wanted her to hate them. They wanted her to do something.

Fireworks sizzled in front of her. Lights swirled in her green irises as she sipped her wine and let it sit on her tongue for a moment.

She had killed before. Killed for love. Killed

because she craved it and lusted for it and some part of her even felt like she *deserved* it. She had killed because she wanted it too much. Because she was selfish. They called her a witch. Tried to burn her at the stake.

But she survived. Eleanor Beaumont always survived.

She flicked open her pocket watch and glanced down at the time. Seven o'clock. She would need to head down to the graveyard soon to host the vigil for Count Lucien. She tilted her head to the sound of footsteps, fingers tightening around her wine glass.

"Lady Beaumont." A servant with a letter in his white-gloved grasp.

Eleanor took it, flipped it over and unfolded it.

How insensitive, it read, *to hold your narcissistic ball tonight?*

She did not even read the full thing, handing it back to the servant and telling him to destroy it. She had read enough of their letters. She would not bow down to the pressure. She would stand firm, just as she always had, just as the Black Dime had taught her. *They will try to undermine me,* she thought as the servant walked away and the sky ripped open with colour. *But I will not budge.*

She walked back into her chambers and glanced

at the hulking suit of armour that stood in the corner. Guillaume peered out at her with his zombie eyes. She walked from him to a shelf where she plucked a voodoo doll. It was Laurent, the man who had come by her manor house the previous day. She was sure he was involved. Why else would he want an alliance? And to sacrifice so much? No. She knew men like him. She caressed the doll with her hands, taking hold of his shoulder joint.

We'll kill every last witch in Bellvoir, one letter had said.

Eleanor Beaumont carried the doll to the open windows of her balcony and stood there, feeling the cold breeze wash over her. She raised the doll to the starlight and gently rolled its shoulder blade. She could hurt him. Bad.

No. That was not their way.

We were vicious, once, she had said some time ago. *We murdered those who stood in our way, who crossed our paths with cutthroat glances. We do not do that anymore. There shall be no more blood on the hands of the witches of Bellvoir.*

And yet the longing for spilt blood made her weak.

She sat the doll down on the windowsill and walked off. Guillaume watched her go, his hand on the hilt of his massive dented broadsword. Servants eyed her warily but none moved, none made so much as a squeak. Lady Beaumont simply strolled from the halls of her manor house and headed for the graveyard vigil.

And in a small tenement down the street, Laurent let out a gasp that was not in pleasure, climbing out of the king-sized bed and brushing sweat from his brow. He walked across the room, butt-naked, rolling his shoulder, which was suddenly aching.

"Is everything alright?" the other man asked.

Laurent cursed between pants.

"Perhaps we should continue this another night?" the man offered. Laurent was reminded of everything he had to lose, of all the puzzle pieces he'd laid down and of all the people he could hurt if he—or *they*—were foolish enough to slip up. But all for the greater good.

"No," Laurent said as he glanced through the small window, which perfectly framed the house of Eleanor Beaumont in all its stark blackness. It couldn't be, could it? Had he had too much to drink? They were just rumours . . . weren't they?

A sigh came from the naked man in his bed.

Laurent caught the sweat on his brow before it dripped into his eyes and then turned around, shaking

Eleanor Beaumont from his thoughts. "Where were we, then?"

"Your cock in my butt, I believe."

"Ah, yes."

———

CELESTE STOOD ACROSS THE ROAD FROM THE Black Dime Cabaret, staring at the pool of red light that drooled out from its open door. A young couple was touching and kissing under the lantern of an apothecary and Celeste ignored them by focusing on the light and the cigarette tucked between her teeth.

She felt odd. Somewhat numb. Somewhat unwell.

My great grandfather didn't kill himself, she thought, remembering the stories they'd told her, what they'd led her to believe. Had they lied, or did they not know? That her great grandfather had been murdered by a woman called Rosalie Beaumont in 1815 and his bastard daughter had fallen to Maria, now the oldest woman in Bellvoir.

Rosalie stole her great grandfather's book on witchcraft. Then she had paved the way for Eleanor Beaumont's birth. The Beaumont blood was in both Celeste and . . .

Lady Eleanor Beaumont herself, queen of the Black Dime.

But what did that mean? Did it mean anything at all?

"Celeste, I'm ready!" Léa said, emerging from the apothecary with a brown bag that clattered with glass vials. "Let's go to the graveyard."

They walked abreast through the town.

"How is she doing?" Léa asked.

Celeste stole a glance at her. Léa's strawberry blonde hair shone under the starlight. The frequency of fireworks had decreased to the point of one exploding in the sky every couple of minutes, but one did erupt now, burning her eyes with green, blue and gold. "Who?"

"Maria. She hasn't been well, from what I've heard."

Celeste thought back to the old woman in the attic, how her nightgown had hung loose and her skin moved like waves and her wrinkles cast shadows, and her voice, her eyes. They had opened and she had told her about Rosalie Beaumont, and that image had burned itself into Celeste's mind. One blind eye, the other pupil horribly displaced.

"Are you okay?" Léa asked.

"Yes, of course. Do I not look okay?" She blew

out a mist of smoke and watched it sail to the sky, drifting through a red lamp. She disliked the taste immeasurably. It reminded her too much of the war. She tossed the cigarette to the ground and crushed it with the heel of her shoe. An autumn leaf fluttered by her foot and she kicked it.

Léa watched her suspiciously, her bag of offerings clanking. Typical items for the vigil. Candles and potions and various non-magical charms, all for the deceased founder of the Black Dime. She accepted Celeste's somewhat aggressive response and the two continued walking, following a dirt path lined with gardens and trees that had been stripped by the autumn climate. Paper lanterns dangled from ropes that were tied between the trees, rustling in the light breeze. Other people walked around them, cheerful and lively, in stupors from the festivities. Léa glanced at Celeste again. "Do you know why we celebrate this night?"

"Is it related to Count Lucien?"

Léa nodded. "He died tonight, more than one hundred years ago."

Celeste felt a spike of tension, an urge to say what was on her mind. "What would it mean," she said, "if my great grandfather didn't kill himself after all?"

"You mean what if he was murdered?"

The suggestion was too quick, like she'd been thinking about it already. "Maria said he was killed by a woman called Rosalie Beaumont who stole everything from him."

They stopped underneath a tree as a red leaf floated between them. Léa briefly considered why Maria would have any reason to lie, and then realised she wouldn't. "So the blood in you is the same blood in Lady Beaumont herself," Léa said.

Celeste nodded.

That's not good, Léa thought but did not mention it. Instead, she continued walking down the graveyard road and did not say another word. A mass of witches had already arrived, all dressed in black and lit only by the dim light of candles.

A bat flew overhead, leaving falling leaves in its wake. The congregation was small, the bat observed, but significant. Perched on top of a lamp post which flickered intermittently, it chirped and detected several more bats and animals emerging from the darkness. The witches talked softly to one another in low, susurrus voices. The bat moved from its position so as to hear them better, landing atop the gated fence that surrounded the graveyard. From here the bat could make out the faded inscription on the gravestone:

Edgar Lucien. 1768-1815.
A kind man adored by all.
Rest in peace.

The bat snickered.

Celeste stared at the bat as she followed Léa through the cemetery gates into the mist that rolled along the dirt ground, weaving about the headstones and shrines. The bat stopped licking itself and then slowly turned its head to look at her, before darting into the shadows. *What are you doing here?* Celeste wondered as it disappeared.

What are you *doing here, dull girl?*

She froze. That voice was not her own.

She spun around and looked up, shielding her eyes from the exuberant light of a flickering lamp post. There was another bat perched on top of it, its wings engulfing its tiny black body.

Mind your own business, the bat said into her mind. This one was a chirpy female voice, aged and shrill. It seemed to be coming from directly inside her own head and she flinched at the immense discomfort. The bat on the lamp post flew away and she spotted another one sitting on a headstone inscribed with: RÉGINE THIBAULT.

How are you talking to me? Celeste asked.

How do you talk to anyone? the bat responded.

Such a rude thing to ask, came a growl that she knew to be behind her. She shot a furtive look beyond Léa towards a small feline statue standing in the grass. Two red eyes peered out of a bush, occasionally blinking. This voice was not a woman's voice, but a deep bass of a man, so deep she could hear his vocal cords bubbling. *What is her name?*

Celeste! came a shout from above.

Celeste looked but there was nothing there, just falling leaves. She moved from the spot, following Léa deeper into the gathering of witches and out of the cold, into the heat from the firepits. And yet, despite this she shivered harder than she had all night.

What a pretty name, cackled a bat sitting on a cross.

Please stop talking to me, Celeste thought back at it, willing the voices to stop. She plugged a finger in her ear but they only became louder in the absence of noise.

She's Count Lucien's, purred the creature with red eyes. It was following her, darting between the shadows to avoid the lights. It seemed very large, every movement causing the bushes to convulse. Could nobody else see this except for her?

The thing with red eyes shrank back into the bushes as Celeste slipped into the crowd of witches, at last feeling that warmth return. But the thing with the red eyes wasn't gone entirely. It remained, watching that odd girl through the crowd. Fresh blood. Celeste. The creature sat on its haunches as more witches arrived and blocked her from sight.

"You look like you've just heard terrible news," Léa said.

The human voice alarmed her and she jumped.

"You're so jumpy. Have the animals been talking to you?"

"What? No, that's ridiculous. Animals don't talk."

Léa smiled. "They're actually not animals. They're just people who are visiting from elsewhere in the world. Vampires. Travelling witches. The Black Dime is larger than you think. We're all over the world. In London. In the heart of New York City itself. Flight is a fast means of transport so they transfigure themselves into animals to get around."

Celeste glanced at one of the large headstones by Lucien's to see two bats perched on top, not moving, just staring at Edgar Lucien's shrine. A frog croaked on the edge of the footpath. An owl peered out from the canopy of a tree, hooting. "They knew my name."

That's odd, Léa thought but did not mention it.

"We've known for a while you would arrive here," she said instead.

"Weird," Celeste said in a soft voice. She wrapped her arms around herself as a cold breeze whispered through the cemetery, lifting dirt from the ground and nudging pebbles that had become lodged between the stone footpath.

Fireworks erupted overhead, splashing red light across the graveyard. Celeste flinched, then let out a deep breath and watched frost fill the space before her. With the corner of her eye she saw a tall figure approaching, her long black dress swirling around her. The woman surveyed the witches, slowing her approach as she neared Count Lucien's shrine. Celeste tried to avoid the woman's eyes but it was impossible. So beautiful. So alluring. It was almost . . . unnatural that one could possess so much beauty and yet she did. The woman was accompanied by three others who also wore black, but with veils over their heads.

"That's Lady Beaumont," Léa said softly.

"And who are those people with her?" Celeste asked.

"Her wardens," Léa said, staring at those three veiled women who walked beside Lady Beaumont, their black eyes glinting under the slivers of moonlight tearing through the skeletal trees. Even Léa, for as long as she'd been a member of the Black Dime, felt miniscule in their presence. "They are the strongest among us. Once, just one of them was able to murder sixteen people simultaneously. She tried then to kill Eleanor too."

"What happened?" Celeste asked, keeping her eyes on Eleanor Beaumont.

Léa said nothing for a moment. "The Exile."

"The Exile?" The word felt heavy and wrong.

"The worst punishment a witch can receive. It has only happened once."

The Exile, Celeste thought. The word caused her to shiver and she didn't dare think of what it entailed, what those wardens, what *Eleanor* was capable of.

Eleanor Beaumont stepped into the circle of light surrounding Count Lucien's shrine, her raven hair blowing in the cold night breeze. She seemed so poised, hands clasped gently, dress billowing, her wardens standing around her with their veiled faces. She glanced momentarily in Celeste's direction and Celeste felt as if she'd been stuck with a pin.

"Thank you for joining me here tonight," Eleanor said. "I feel that it is important we continue to remember and acknowledge those who laid down the foundations of what we are today. Our history is one of great importance. Those who have come before us have paved the way for a rich history of traditions and family which will continue to thrive long after I'm gone, long after any of us are gone. To be a witch in France is to be independent from the outer world. To have a place to call home even in the worst of times."

Eleanor's eyes glided across the shadowy group. "Our history is muddled, oftentimes nonsensical, but there is one certainty hidden amongst all the confusion, and that is that we are here today because of one man. Edgar Lucien."

Bats squawked overhead and a shard of moonlight reflected off the inscription on Lucien's eroding shrine. Celeste felt her breath be sucked from her lungs as she stared at it, imagining the bones buried underneath it. How much did they all *really* know about Edgar Lucien? How much of his history was just as befuddled as the rest of the Black Dime?

"It was written," Eleanor continued, "that as he sensed his own death approaching, the Count of Bellvoir—Edgar Lucien himself—donated two thirds of his entire wealth into the Black Dime and the parts of Bellvoir that needed it the most. It was said that two days before his death, he visited the estate of his greatest critic and offered him the large sum of money he needed in order to fund his own personal art projects. When he spent six years in Italy studying sorcery from Rita Galeazzi in the institution in Matera, he did it with the very same ambition and hunger for knowledge that still lives in all witches today."

A bat who was sitting on top of a broken headstone chuckled. He remembered when Edgar Lucien began donating his wealth. Such a thing had been unprecedented! The papers adored him for it, helped burnish his legacy in golden sheen. But did anybody know this man at all?

Well, the answer was simple. Nobody *really* knew Count Lucien, not back then and certainly not now, nearly eighty years following his death. But in life he had had a way with words, a way with *people,* how he could so easily bend popular opinion to his will.

"Lunacy!" exclaimed Edgar Lucien, slamming his fist into the table at the back of the gentleman's club as half-naked women strolled around them, pouring drinks. "It is damned outrageous that I should be forced to give him so much of my wealth! Have you lost your mind?"

The man who sat opposite Lucien was the father of the man who now watched the graveyard scene in the form of a bat, a balding man called Jules with more moustache than hair and responsible for producing more smoke from his cigars than all the chimneys in Bellvoir combined. His smoking habit would kill him in three months, suddenly and brutally. "No, Edgar, I have not lost my mind." He coughed into a white serviette, checking it for blood. It was clean, thank god. "You may not like him, but you owe that man that money."

"He can pick it off my corpse!" Lucien blurted. A showgirl pranced up to him and gently caressed his chest. Lucien whipped back his elbow and struck her in the ribs, causing the girl to shriek as she flew to the ground. "Don't bloody touch me, you worthless whore!" Lucien screamed, kicking back his chair and sending dust and wood flying into the air. The woman stared at him with her mouth agape, and scuttled off.

"Good lord, Lucien, what the hell are you doing?" Jules said.

"I don't pay to feed my enemies," Lucien said. "That's all they ever do, pick up the scraps of my success. Well here's something for you, Jules, those scraps don't belong to them!"

"You don't bloody own this town, Edgar!"

"Piss off!" Edgar screamed, standing with such force his chair flew back into another table. By now, they'd attracted quite the crowd. Edgar stared down at Jules, his large figure casting an extraordinary and intimidating shadow across the bar.

Jules tore out his cigar and spat out the smoke.

"Well don't let me stop you. Go forth and do as you will, go see what happens, but this world's not yours, Edgar! The consequences come for you just as they come for the rats in the gutter. So then don't pay this man. Forget the people who helped you get to where you are now and drink your wine in your own sequestered quarters. They will remember you, Edgar, and if I were you I'd do something fast so they don't remember you as you are in this moment. How *embarrassing*."

Jules jammed his cigar back into his mouth and walked out.

"Come back here!" Lucien slammed the table with his fist.

Only Jules knew who the Count really was. There were rumours, sure, but there were always rumours, and always so many that they came to mean nothing in the end. Italy changed things. When Edgar went to Italy in 1788 and met that woman, Rita Galeazzi, that was when he changed. But nobody knew what really happened there. Nobody *would*.

Only the Count of Bellvoir himself knew the truth.

How he'd entered Rita's quarters at six minutes past midnight, all dark except the faint glimmer of moonlight that shone through her arched window. He had expected to find her asleep but she was standing in the moonlight, her raven hair laced like cobwebs on her shoulders, her white nightgown becoming almost translucent under the harsh moon's gaze.

How he'd stood there in the shadows, seeing how the silver light split in two parts around Rita's dark figure, shining across the room in all the places Edgar was not.

"You have come here to kill me," Rita said.

"No, of course not," Edgar said softly.

Rita turned to face him, her long hair falling across her right eye. Her other one had an unnatural red glow to it. Her expression was placid and unjudging. "I have known since you first arrived here at the institution three years ago what you would do. This has given me time to think it over, perhaps more so than even you have. I would not attempt it."

Edgar hesitated, his knife concealed in the darkness.

"Why did you come here in the first place?" Rita asked.

"You know why I'm here," Edgar growled. A gust of wind slapped against the window and the curtains were tossed back dramatically.

"I do not have the answers you seek," Rita said.

"Liar!" Edgar yelled, his fingers twitching around the haft of his knife. "All this research, all the questions and the answers, is it all meaningless to you? I have everything, Rita—everything! I will expose your games and your lies and this secret society, I swear it—"

Something gripped him around the throat and his knife clattered to the floor. He folded to his knees, grappling at his windpipe. Edgar let out a choke as he looked up at the woman who stood in the moonlight, so poised, so beautiful.

"It is admirable what you have done," Rita said. "I must say, your dedication to the pursuit of knowledge has impressed me. There's no point in keeping secrets. In fact, I do not fear word of witches in Italy getting out. You're not the first to come here."

Edgar tried to speak but he couldn't breathe.

Rita stepped closer to him. "But don't fool yourself, Edgar, you're no sorcerer. You may possess the knowledge and the history and you may have *his* name but you don't have his power. It's pathetic, really, how despite your desperation you've failed so miserably."

"Who . . . am I?" Edgar pleaded, veins in his throat pulsating.

"It is true, your father was Odilon Lucien but why should that make you anybody significant? You're just Edgar, a man who knows too much and who doesn't belong, not in your pathetic world and not in the one he so desperately wishes to be a part of."

Edgar began to laugh, and then cackle, and then he released his hands from his throat and lay on the floor cackling under the moonlight.

Rita watched him, unnerved.

Not too far outside her chambers, fourth-year student of the institution, a girl by the name of Laura Schiaparelli, felt the air go numb and it was enough to raise the hairs on the back of her neck. She poked her head out of her dorm room and peered down the hall, into the deep silence, knitting equipment still in her hand and a loose thread dangling to the floor. The air had gone stiff. *Someone has died,* she thought.

Moments later, a scream echoed through the institution.

Laura ran into the common room just as the fire in the hearth died, coughing out black char. She gave a yelp. The double doors on the other side of the room swung open and in barged Natale, tripping over the threshold in her nightgown.

"What is happening?" Laura said with panic.

"Help me!" Natale screamed as she ran into Laura's arms, flailing her wrist. Laura, who was knowledgeable about many things in the witching texts, took hold of her friend's arm and immediately felt a rush of dread. Her arm was swelling with veins, turning purple and then black and then the skin began to warp as her arm collapsed in on itself. Natale screamed in absolute agony, dropping with Laura to her knees. At this point, other students had run into the common room. Natale's arm folded in on itself, and then her chest, like somebody was crushing her in between gigantic, ghostly arms, like she were made of paper and not flesh. She screamed, blood splashing across Laura and the carpet of the common room.

The doors were flung open again and Laura looked up as a male student revealed a flintlock pistol and shot Natale through the back. Then he shot Laura. Then he shot another student.

And meanwhile, the same thing was happening in another room.

And gunshots rang out from classrooms. And dorms.

In a room deep within the labyrinthine walls of the institution of witchcraft in Matera, somewhere within the mountains of Italy, Edgar Lucien sat down on Rita Galeazzi's bed, his shoulders slumped, shaking to his core, as blood oozed out of the body of the woman on the floor, twisted and burnt like no body should ever be.

"When he returned," Eleanor Beaumont said now,

one hundred and two years later, in the graveyard of Bellvoir, surrounded by witches and animals, including one bat who had been the son of Jules, who had been the only person who knew the truth about the Count of Bellvoir, "Edgar Lucien imparted his knowledge on a new order of witches, one that continues to thrive to this day. May he ever rest in peace, and may we all strive to live up to his name."

The next thirty minutes consisted of the witches making offerings to Eleanor Beaumont and the shrine of Edgar Lucien. Celeste watched from the graveyard gates, not partaking. And all the while, a bat stood over her shoulder.

This is the one, the bat thought.

Who is it? another thought into its mind.

The one who scares me.

Only when Celeste had left the graveyard did the bat finally leave, chirping as it ascended through the streams of moonlight into the canopy of a tree, and then out of Bellvoir.

VIII

ANOTHER DEAD MAN

his is a mess," said the short, stout detective as he took off his hat and stared up at the dangling shoes of a man who'd hung himself so poorly his neck was hanging by tendons. A wooden box had been flung out a few feet away, suggesting he'd launched himself off that. The entire left side of his body, naked but for grey suit pants, was drenched in blood.

The clown watched it from the edge of the second-floor bedroom by the window, feeling the heat of the morning sun against his back. "How long's he been here?"

The detective, Granger, paced around the body

in a circle. The room was in a fairly orderly state. Expensive. Some might even say ostentatious. He was hanging from a glass chandelier and his bed was perfectly made. Nothing was out of place except for the dead man himself.

"He died last night," Granger said.

The clown threw his hands into his overlarge pockets and walked slowly to the dead man. This was very bad. First Gustave Mathieu, shot to death in the dark of night, then this man. Julien Lémieux. The clown slipped out a folded-up letter that was poking out of the man's pocket, the edge of it stained with blood that still ran wet.

"May I ask what's with the clown outfit?" Granger said in his pinched voice.

The clown glanced at him, airing out the letter so that the wet droplets of blood transferred onto the dusty floorboards. "I guess I'm just overenthusiastic about my job."

The real answer was he was stuck in the damn thing.

Granger took his response as weird but there were weird men in Bellvoir so he didn't question it. There were bigger problems, such as the man dangling from the chandelier. He watched the clown open the letter, keeping it away from his painted face as he read what it contained.

"What's it say?" Granger said.

"It's just a boring suicide letter," the clown said, handing the note to the detective. The door creaked open and two more officers entered, one man and a woman, both in uniform. Behind them was an elderly woman in a pink nightgown, her eyes red and her gaunt face laced with tears. When she saw the dead man she screamed and the female officer promptly escorted her out, slamming the door shut behind them.

"Jesus Christ," the male officer said. He revealed a badge, which glinted in the sunlight. "Chief Alphonse Delacroix." With moderate degree of theatre, the man stowed his badge and rapped his knuckle against the hanging man's pale wrist. "Dead stiff. Who was he?"

Granger perked up. "An election candidate. Julien Lémieux."

"Next of kin? That old woman?"

"No family of note. Don't know who she was."

Chief Delacroix glanced at the letter. "Give me that." Granger handed it to him and Delacroix opened it up, gave it a quick look. "Boring suicide letter." The clown watched him and waited for the inevitable question of what led to the man's death, if there were sinister undertones, if it was in any way connected to the death of Gustave Mathieu two nights ago.

Where was the blame on the witches?

"You think it could be related to the Mathieu murder?" Granger said.

There it was.

"I wouldn't rule it out," Delacroix said. "Look at him. Wealthy men don't just kill themselves, especially not in the midst of an important election."

"Is that so?" said the clown.

Delacroix looked at him, bemused. "What is your business here, clown man?"

"I'm the one who found the body."

"Hm," Delacroix said thoughtfully. They all looked at the hanging man, who turned slightly in the breeze. "Perhaps a witch influenced his decision. What's her name in her manor house? Eleanor Beaumont. The witch who brought the plague."

Damn. The clown could not imagine a situation that was worse than this, with the Mathieu murder and now this one, tension in Bellvoir had never been worse. If word of Lemieux's death got out, the consequences could be devastating. It was the last thing that raven man needed to rally a lynch mob and burn down the entire town—all over rumours.

A tyrant was born in the gutter, he recalled. The

prophecy of the man who would burn down France had followed the clown everywhere he went. After nearly eighty years, the prophecy was finally coming to light. The circumstances were all so unlikely and horrible that it couldn't possibly be anything else. This was fate—a terrible, terrible fate.

"We'd best keep this secret," Chief Delacroix said.

"The skeleton man," Granger said as he sat down on the wooden box that the man had jumped from to hang himself. "What if it's him? The one who's always singing?"

Chief Delacroix looked at him. "What the hell are you talking about? There's no bloody skeleton man around here, you idiot."

There was a sickening rip and the body fell, splashing in the blood on the floorboards. Granger yelped, jumping to his feet. Delacroix athletically leapt away from it. One second later, the head fell with a dull thud on top of the lifeless body.

"That's certifiably disgusting," Delacroix noted.

"I'll call the clean-up crews," Granger said.

The clown and Delacroix looked at each other, the headless body between them. There was a tapping sound, Delacroix's shoe on the wet floorboards.

"Do you believe there are witches?" Delacroix said.

"I believe there are witches but I don't believe they're killing election candidates," the clown said. "What does Lady Beaumont gain by murdering half the town?"

Delacroix thought about this for a moment. "I suppose it's in the best interest of everybody that we keep this a secret. We announce that Mister Lémieux here withdrew from the campaign. In fact, he's alive and quite well. He's in Paris, actually."

"Of course," the clown said.

"You should head back home," Delacroix said, and the clown was satisfied. With one last glance at the poor body, half naked and headless, he turned on his heel and left the building.

THE CHURCH BELLS WERE RINGING AS THE CLOWN walked past the house of Celeste Lucien and then through the marketplace with his hands in his pockets and his head down. He purchased a few sticks of bread and thought a cheese and olive sandwich would go down nicely.

He returned to the tenements where he was staying and sat inside his study, drawing the curtain open to let in the mid-morning light. There he poured himself some white wine and nibbled on a sandwich as he pulled out a blank sheet of paper and wrote.

Dear Raven Man.

His pen lifted from the page and he stared at those words, pensive. He had to play this safe. Keep his cards close to his chest. Offer no new information, nothing that could make the situation worse. He could certainly not tell the raven man about these latest developments.

Taking a sip of wine, he drew his pen back to the page.

I'm writing to warn you of the potential consequences of starting a war against the witches of Bellvoir, he wrote, slowly and carefully. *Remember, the prophecy. Remember the tyrant who was born in the gutter. I believe I mean no disrespect by saying these words appear eerily ominous.*

The clown was not permitted to overtly alter the natural course of events, but he could give things a little bit of a . . . *push* if he deemed it necessary. In this case it was absolutely necessary, for if the raven man went through with his plan, it would be catastrophic.

Pressing the ink tip to the page, he continued to write . . .

Across the town in an empty chapel, dark except for the rays of light that twinkled like ballet dancers through the rose-glass windows, the raven man sat on a pew gazing forward at the vacant altar. A man was sitting behind a piano playing a sad melody. A few feet away from Regis, on his right and in the shadow, stood a man with raven feathers growing out of his neck and a raven mask covering his face.

In his hands he held a letter and he read from it now.

" 'I beg you,' " read the man in the raven mask with a coarse voice, " 'whatever it is you seek to achieve in the coming days, I beg you not to try anything that would break the momentary peace we have achieved between the worlds of witches and man.' "

Regis stared at the altar as the music played and the man spoke to him. A glint of light flashed across the weapon in his hands—a black dagger, the length of his forearm. In its hilt was an emerald stone and an ancient inscription that read:

CE POIGNARD ASSASSINE DES SORCIÈRES

" 'Lady Beaumont is innocent,' " read the man. " 'Not her nor any other witch in Bellvoir is responsible for any murders in this town. I say this only because I care about France and I fear you do not quite understand how far this action will ripple out, the consequences of it. I suppose the decision is yours to make. I cannot stop you, only advise, but I have never advised anybody with more sincerity than I advise you now: Do not murder Lady Beaumont.' "

There was the crinkling of paper as the man folded it up.

Regis turned the dagger in his hands, feeling the cold black steel with his smooth fingertips. The words of the mysterious sender swirled through his head. He imagined coming face-to-face with Eleanor Beaumont, putting the dagger in her heart and watching her drop to the floor. Witches caused the plague that was feasting on the people in the gutter. Witches murdered Gustave Mathieu in cold blood.

For too long they had been left unchecked.

If Regis was to be this tyrant in the gutter, then so be it. But he would much prefer that than to see the day France becomes obliterated by witches and their vicious ways.

"I want you to call for the ravens," Regis said as he touched the edge of the dagger, drawing the slightest bead of blood, which began to slowly streak down the blade. He could not begin to doubt himself. He was either completely in or he was out, because he knew that if he allowed even the slightest tinge of doubt to creep in, everything would fail.

That's what they're trying to do, he thought. *They want me to doubt myself. They want me to ask the very same questions I've spent years answering for myself. I won't do it.*

"Tell them tonight, Lady Midnight dies," Regis said.

The man in the mask nodded. "Praise the Raven."

"It is praised," Regis replied. The man in the mask departed just as the man on the piano finished his song with a flourish of keys. Regis did not move, listening to the tail of the music reverberate through the chapel, until all that remained was the memory of it. The melody had nearly faded from his mind when a new one began, slow and depressing.

Regis drew a deep breath as he stood, extending his arms to the side, spreading his fingers and waving the dagger. He drifted into the light streaming in through the main arched window, watching the motes of dust tumble away from him.

How sweet it will be, he thought, *when there are no more witches in Bellvoir.*

He tiptoed forward, then struck out into a killing pose, the dagger splitting the air before him. His black coat flailed outwards, theatrical. Regis held the pose, then retreated.

No more plague. He mimed grabbing Lady Midnight by the shoulder and ramming the dagger through her ribs. *No more conspiracies.* He mimed kicking out with his boot and striking her back legs, sending her crumpling to the floor. *No more war!* He strolled past the imaginary place where she sat, weeping, slashing through the air with his dagger as if slashing through her neck. He imagined the sound of her body thumping to the floor. *No more injustice!*

He slid the dagger into the sheathe he wore from his belt.

He withdrew a pocket watch from his coat and flipped it open, his breath tremoring. There was sweat in his hands, which smudged the cold steel of the pocket watch. It ticked slowly, echoing through the chapel. Eleven fifteen.

THE BELLS OF MIDDAY RANG OUT AND CHRISTOPHE Archambault was pacing back and forth in his office, reading the latest newspaper in one hand and holding a jam croissant with the other. He was giggling at the political cartoons that Michel Baudin drew three times a week. The man was a genius when it came to satirising the intricacies of the election and Archambault would certainly miss him when the election came to an end in the coming weeks.

There was a knock on his door.

"Come in," Archambault called out.

The door swung open and in walked Sophie, a stack of letters in her arms. She kicked the door shut behind her and dumped the letters on Archambault's desk. Archambault walked up to her as he took a chunk out of his croissant, glancing at the pile.

"You know you could just burn those letters," Archambault said.

"The town would appreciate it if they at least believed you read them," Sophie said with a smile on her plump pink lips as she grabbed his shirt and kissed him hard.

Archambault withdrew, revealing his croissant. "This is nothing against you. In fact, you look gorgeous today, but these croissants are unfairly good."

"Wait too long and I'll change my mind," Sophie said, her breath against his face as she took hold of his tie and began playing with it. Archambault tossed the croissant into his mouth and tossed the newspaper at his desk, missing entirely.

He'd barely swallowed the croissant when Sophie threw herself at him and he kissed her, his hands tangled in her sweet locks of caramel hair. She smashed him against a cabinet, causing one of the drawers to fly out and smack him in the back of the head. A hand swept out and grabbed the cord for the curtains, yanking it down and plunging the room in darkness.

Sophie was an enigma, entering his life at the most opportune moment right at the dawn of the election campaign and softening him up just a little bit. Their relationship had moved fast, and it was only three days before Sophie was gasping for more.

"Christophe," said a man as he walked into the room.

"What do you want?" Archambault responded, fiddling with the knots on Sophie's blouse. He gazed past the bloom of Sophie's hair at the man who stood in the doorway, a black binder in his hand. The man was Constant, one of his advisors.

"Um, if it isn't too much to ask could you stop that?"

Archambault groaned as Sophie kissed the edge of his lips and he freed her stubborn dress to reveal the flowery material of her bra. She gave out a moan as she began stripping off his belt. "What is it, Constant? I told you to direct enquiries to Irma's office!"

Constant sighed, removing his reading glasses and scratching the hook of his nose as Archambault and the girl carried on in the corner by the filing cabinets. He had to admit, he did not like Sophie very much—she was *far* too intent on him. "This is a matter of reasonable importance and I thought you'd be interested in hearing it directly."

"Could it wait?" Archambault said as their fiasco went on.

"No," Constant said from the doorway, maintaining strong eye contact.

"Very well, but I'm warning you, this had better be extraordinary news."

"Well does another dead man strike you as being extraordinary news?" Constant said, giddy to reveal the information. Archambault was a somewhat difficult man to please if you were not a woman several decades younger than himself, but Constant knew what the man liked, knew the only thing he liked more than women was front page exclusives.

For the briefest moment, Archambault's mind drifted from the girl to Constant's latest revelation. "Who died?"

Constant smirked. "Candidate Julien Lémieux. At his home. He hung himself so poorly that his neck split and his head came off. My contact sent me a forged copy of his suicide letter, which suggests foul play. I wouldn't want to speculate, but an awful lot of election candidates have been dropping dead lately, and the polls are shifting extraordinarily."

"What do the polls say?" Archambault said.

"That Eleanor Beaumont is growing in popularity," Constant said.

"Why the bloody hell would that be?"

"I suppose people really do despise politicians."

"Goddammit, leak the information!" He shoved Sophie out of the way and she gave out a chicken-like yelp. Doing up his pants buttons and then his belt, he said, "Tell them that Eleanor Beaumont doesn't intend on stopping with the politicians. She's coming for them next. Write this: The Black Dime is full of witches and everybody knows the witches caused the plague."

"Of course," Constant said.

Archambault tidied himself up, combing back his luscious blond hair. He stood alarmingly close to Constant, a looming presence over him. Behind them, Sophie fixed her bra and her blouse and brushed back her own hair, watching the men. Archambault lowered his voice. "What are they saying happened to him? What lie did they make to cover it up?"

"Well the lie was that he's gone to Paris."

Archambault laughed raucously. "Now *that's* a good one!"

"It does show that people will believe anything considering he would have required an unfound method of teleportation to reach Paris in such a span of time."

"Stop, you're hurting my intelligence."

"Laurent went to Paris too," Sophie blurted.

Archambault and Constant looked at her at the same time.

"Is that so?" Archambault mused, scratching his chin. He glanced at Constant, who looked back with a thoughtful expression, having to stop a moment to think.

Sophie nodded eagerly.

"Why would Laurent go to Paris?" Archambault said.

"He—" she started.

"It would make sense," Constant interrupted thoughtfully. "Laurent has always had a fondness for theatre and this is the time when he is wont to depart on such trips."

Archambault nodded. To be honest, he was glad Laurent was not in Bellvoir at this time. The man was the living manifestation of a headache. They had not spoken in years, had barely even seen each other, but election time always saw Laurent ascend his list of annoyances.

"Thank you for giving me this information," Archambault said. "I will have it in the papers by the end of the day." Constant bowed his head and then departed the room. The curtains were flung open and Archambault squinted, shielding his eyes.

Sophie was staring at him hotly.

"My apologies," Archambault said.

"Take a look at those letters, would you?" Sophie said as she tied back her gorgeous hair and started walking back to the door. "I think they'll be of some interest to you. Particularly the one on top."

"Anything for you," Archambault said, watching her leave.

When the door shut behind her, he strolled to his desk and picked up the first letter on the pile. It bore an expensive red stamp and had his name written on the front in very nice cursive. Frowning, he slashed it open and unfolded the letter inside.

You are invited, read the letter.

To the annual ball of Eleanor Beaumont.

Doors open at 7pm. The Lady looks forward to seeing you there.

Archambault looked from the letter to the window and the sprawling town below him. He had known he would receive an invitation—the upper class was always invited to Eleanor Beaumont's annual ball—but something this year felt different.

Were the rumours of witches in Bellvoir true?

He smiled, and figured he would not miss this for anything.

LAURENT, WHO WAS ABSOLUTELY NOT IN PARIS, HAD seen the guest list for Eleanor Beaumont's annual ball tonight so when the invitation came in the mail he had already informed Ferdinand and had picked out suits for both of them. He was sitting on the balcony of his private estate drinking tea and reading the newspaper, gazing out at the distant house of the Lady herself.

If something was going to happen, it would happen tonight. There was too much tension and unrest in the city for something *not* to happen. All he had to do was stay in Eleanor Beaumont's good will. Presently it didn't matter whether she was a witch or not, although Laurent was starting to think that maybe she was. All that mattered was Laurent did not get involved in any greater capacity than he deemed necessary—and that meant Ferdinand too.

He took a sip from his hot ceramic cup of tea. Eleanor Beaumont did put on the most spectacular balls.

He glanced at his pocket watch. Ten past one.

———⟡———

THEODORE MATHIEU, THE ELDEST SON OF THE murdered Gustave Mathieu, sat on a park bench directly outside the Black Dime Cabaret, watching performers walk in and out. He had been sitting there ever since the invitation landed on his desk. A pity invitation, he suspected, as a way to make peace with him or to pretend she cared about him or his dead father.

Doors open at 7pm, the letter had read.

The Lady looks forward to seeing you there.

Theodore had barely avoided bursting out into laughter. The tenacity of that woman, to invite the eldest son of the man she outright murdered!

Oh, he could not wait to meet her.

A raven landed on the bench beside him, an envelope lodged between its stark black beak. The raven eyed him as he carefully plucked this envelope, looked at the onyx seal. He opened it up and read the words it contained, scribbled in haste that very morning by a man who wore a raven mask. The raven watched him closely as he read the letter, sensing a fire begin to broil in the young man's gut. The raven had been there when the letter was written, had seen the eyes of the man who wrote it.

"Give this to the Mathieu boy," the raven man had said as he offered the letter to the raven and then sent it flying out the window of his third-floor study.

Meet me behind the old apothecary's shop, the letter read.

A single name was signed at the bottom: *Regis*.

His watch, which he'd taken from his father's dead body, expensive and embroidered with gold, glinted in the sunlight as it read two thirty in the afternoon.

CELESTE FED HER CAT AND THEN WALKED OUTSIDE the front door of the Lucien estate to the porch, overlooking the lake to the east. She softly inhaled through her nose, soaked in the sounds of chatter and townsfolk shouting their wares.

It was three o'clock in the afternoon and a ferry was approaching across the lake. Celeste could hear a child shouting in delight from the little boat, and she smiled. The roar of a bike alarmed her and a man pulled up with a bag of letters.

"The Lucien estate?" he said to her.

"Yes," she replied.

He handed her a letter with an onyx seal and then

drove off with a friendly smile. Celeste watched him until he was gone. The letter was unexpected. She carefully opened it up as a gust of wind tossed back her blonde hair and yellow dress.

You are invited, it read.

To the annual ball of Eleanor Beaumont.

Doors open at 7pm. The Lady looks forward to seeing you there.

She stared at those words for a long time after reading them, and only when her house door swung open and Nettie meowed, gliding against her calves, did she look up and remember herself. An invitation to Lady Beaumont's ball? Did the Lady know who she was?

Did she know about their connection?

She wasn't sure what to think, except that she ought to get back to the cabaret. Nettie meowed and Celeste glanced at her, watching the tassels of her skirt fly about in the autumn breeze. She knelt down and patted Nettie softly on her furry black head.

"I'll be back soon," Celeste said.

Nettie meowed and watched her leave, headed for the Black Dime Cabaret. There was something wrong with Bellvoir, Nettie thought as she sat down on the dirt and leaves. There was a tremor in the wind, as though something terrible was about to happen.

THE CLOWN STOOD OUTSIDE THE HOUSE OF Eleanor Beaumont, looking up. Tonight, there was the very real possibility of catastrophe. He'd done all he could to prevent it, but the truth was he couldn't really do much but wait, and hope these people of Bellvoir were smarter than they looked.

He slid his hands into his pockets, a cigarette in his mouth spewing smoke into the air. The house of Eleanor Beaumont looked as stagnant and stolid as always, black architecture and red windows, like an expansion of the Black Dime Cabaret itself.

Except tonight was the one night where it all changed, when the house came to life with lights and music and, sometimes, nefarious schemes.

Eleanor Beaumont walked to her fourth floor window and peered out at the street, gazing down at the clown who was looking back at her. She felt the floorboards groan and creak, heard the shifting of heavy metal armour as Guillaume appeared at her side, massive and zombielike with his broadsword sheathed.

"I want you to be on your best behaviour tonight," Eleanor said. Guillaume breathed deeply, his breaths like the purrs of a giant, undead cat.

The clown stared at Eleanor and the giant monstrosity of metal beside her. The clown knew nothing. Not what she was capable of. Not what the raven man was capable of. Not what the politicians were capable of. This unknowing frightened him.

Eleanor wondered who that clown was and why she kept seeing him, but she felt that he should not exist in this world. He was staring at her across the street beneath his pale makeup.

Eleanor stared back and did not move.

IX

NEFARIOUS SCHEMES

éa was smoking a cigarette backstage at the cabaret. The entire room was red, cursed with the smell of sweat and sore bodies. She rested her head back against the wall, blowing a wisp of smoke into the air. The quiet drool of cabaret music murmured through the walls and she listened to it, gently tapping her foot to the beat.

Jacqueline entered from the side door in a black flowery corset, polishing her new venetian masquerade mask, her shoes hanging from her teeth by their laces.

Jacqueline sighed as she spat out her shoes onto a wooden bench on the other side of the room, tossing her masquerade mask on top of them. Her bright eyes glinted in the red lights. "You okay, Léa?" she asked, pulling out a cigarette.

"Cold," she responded.

Jacqueline stared, unsure. Goosebumps prickled her bare skin and she let out a shiver. She opened up her locker and tossed her belongings inside it, exchanging them for a coat and shrugging it on. She crossed the room and pulled aside the black curtain that led out onto the stage. Her twin brother Vincent was performing one of his solos to a minimal crowd. She glanced at the pocket watch that hung from a hook near the curtain. It was five minutes to six.

"What is happening to this town?" Jacqueline said.

The crowd softly applauded as Vincent finished his act and glanced at her. Jacqueline let the curtain fall and walked back inside the backstage room.

"For the first time since I came here," Jacqueline said, standing in the middle of the room and staring at Léa, whose eyes appeared distant and unfocused, "I feel afraid of what's going to happen. They've been saying it's Lady Beaumont who's been murdering all those election candidates. I've been wondering..." She lowered her voice. "What if it's true?" Sickness gripped her stomach as she heard the words leave her lips. Shocked that she could think of such a terrible thing, she drew her cigarette and smoked it fast.

"What if it didn't matter?" Léa said.

"What do you mean?" Jacqueline said.

Vincent entered with a sigh, tossing his violet top hat through the air. It hissed by Jacqueline. He threw his foot onto a bench and began untying his laces.

"I mean," Léa said, "what if it doesn't matter what's true or not because people just believe whatever they read in the papers? This town wants us gone, Jacqueline. Honestly, I don't even know why we're still here. Everybody wants us gone."

"What are you girls talking about?" Vincent said.

Léa threw her cigarette onto the floor and stepped on it. "Nothing. You've read the papers. They want us out of this town. Are you going to the ball tonight? I wouldn't be surprised if they've got it all planned out. They're going to murder Lady Beaumont tonight. You just wait and see." She paused. But what was there to be afraid of? They were witches, weren't they? Lady Beaumont had protection, she had her wardens, she had *them*. "We've forgotten what we are. We are the *Black Dime*. Our blood runs deeper in Bellvoir than any of them, yet they think they can just throw us out like we're rubbish? No. Fuck that."

Jacqueline stared at Léa. "That is not our way."

"We've *lost* our way, Jacqueline," Léa said, her voice ringing through the backstage room. Jacqueline recoiled away from her. "What do you think will happen the moment they're given a reason to slaughter us? What do you think they will do next once Lady Beaumont is gone? Have you any idea how many of them there must be in this town? How many of them hate us? Want us dead?"

"What separates us from the witches of our past is that we don't do that," Jacqueline said. "We only ever use our talents for good."

"They plan to murder us!"

"Oh my god, I know!" Jacqueline shrieked, grabbing her face and walking away. Vincent followed her. "I don't want to be here tonight," Jacqueline said. "I don't want to see it."

"We must fight back," Léa said, lowering her voice.

"What on Earth is happening in here?" Marguerite said as she entered, the curtains erupting around her plump figure. She had her hands on her hips and a pinched look on her face, the red whorls on her cheeks appearing to spin in the tricky light.

Jacqueline debated whether or not she should reveal Léa's plan—reveal the heresy she had spoken. If Marguerite ever knew of such a thing, she would have

Léa banished from the order immediately. Marguerite knew better than anyone the consequences of dark arts.

Marguerite looked from Jacqueline to Léa, then to Vincent, strolling deeper into the room. Léa forced herself to relax her shoulders. Was this where she finally began to lose it? She turned away from Marguerite's intimidating stare and instead began packing her things, shrugging on a coat to head back out into the cold, prepare for the night's proceedings.

"Is everything okay, Léa?" Marguerite said, stopping her in her tracks.

Léa felt a shiver run through her body as she faced the exit, her belongings hanging from her fingertips. She was not sure if Marguerite meant this as a threat or if she was genuinely concerned for her wellbeing. Léa wasn't sure what to tell her. Despite serving tongues of many different forms in the cabaret, the woman was oddly daft. She may not even have been aware in the slightest of the possible murder plot tonight.

Floorboards creaked as Marguerite approached her. "Léa?"

Léa identified kindness in her eyes. Marguerite extended her hand and rested it gently on Léa's shoulder. "It's nothing, Marguerite."

Marguerite did not believe her but accepted her response. Sliding her hand from Léa's shoulder, she said, "Enjoy the rest of your night." Léa left but only after a moment of consideration. She was not entirely sure if she believed that Marguerite was being completely honest with her. Nevertheless, she nodded softly and walked out. Jacqueline and Vincent moved to follow.

"Stay back, Jacqueline," Marguerite said before she reached the door. Both Léa and Vincent stopped, glancing over their shoulders. "Just Jacqueline. You two may leave."

The red room side of stage grew suddenly very cold and quiet. It was the quietest Jacqueline had ever heard the cabaret. There was no music. No voices. No footsteps on the wooden floorboards. Just her and Marguerite and, somewhere, the ticking of a clock.

"What is it?" Jacqueline whispered.

Marguerite stared at her. "Is everything okay?"

NETTIE MEOWED AS LÉA WALKED INTO THE LUCIEN estate, ascending the stairs to Celeste's bedroom. Celeste was standing before the mirror in a bold, blossoming ball gown, evening light streaming through a window and illuminating a path of dust towards her.

Celeste jumped as she saw Léa enter the window's gaze.

"Oh, I'm sorry," Léa said reflexively.

"No it's fine." Celeste patted down the folds in her dress and turned. The dress was everything she could have wanted in one and she could not wait to strut the ballroom in it. Léa walked up behind her, dusting down her shoulders and fixing her blonde hair.

"You look great," Léa said.

"Thank you." Celeste smiled into the mirror. Her cheeks glowed rose. She almost did not recognise herself, and for the first time since before the war, she felt as if she truly belonged somewhere. Léa made a satisfying *hmm* and stood behind her with her hands on Celeste's shoulders. She slid them to her upper arms, straightening the sleeves, and Celeste became acutely aware of her breath against the back of her head. She pointedly avoided Léa's stare in the mirror. "Is everything okay?"

"Of course. I'm sorry." Léa strode away and placed her belongings on the bed, opening one of the large bags to withdraw a black dress, speckled with bits of red. She began to undress and Celeste turned away, walking to the window and staring outside. The evening sun turned the sky a crepuscular purple. It was quite beautiful. She stared forward at the tall estate of Lady Beaumont, completely engulfed in lights.

She played with the pendant she wore around her neck. It was a transparent orb with an opal in it. It had belonged to her mother and that was all she knew about it. Her mother had worn it on her wedding night and it had been found among her possessions when she died.

"Do you think she'd want to meet me?" Celeste asked.

Léa yanked her dress up over herself with more than just a moderate degree of trouble, feeling her breath be constricted by the rather tight corset. She thought about what Celeste had told her the night before in the graveyard. They were blood, her and Lady Beaumont. Not close blood. The link was obscured and very, very distant. It was one scandal at one very specific moment of time that connected them. But they *were* blood.

Léa straightened. "I'm not sure."

Regardless, she thought that perhaps it would be better if Lady Beaumont did not know about Celeste. Or did she already know? How much did Lady Beaumont know about all of this? About how much they hated her? About the fact they might try to kill her?

"I see," Celeste said with some measure of disappointment.

Léa bit her lip. Celeste knew nothing about Bellvoir. She didn't know what the people were capable of. Léa felt that she should tell her, but she could not. "Could you help me with this?" she said. Celeste nodded, slowly wandering over to her and helping her squeeze into the black corset.

Neither of them spoke.

Celeste thought that Léa was hiding something from her but she didn't think to mention it. Instead, she simply smiled and imagined how wonderful this night would be. She stepped away from Léa and eyed her up and down. "You look really good."

Léa smirked. "I know. Can I borrow some of your makeup?"

"Of course," Celeste said, motioning Léa into the other room. Celeste sat down on the edge of her bed and waited in silence, resting her hands in her lap. She pulled out her pocket watch and checked the time.

Eighteen minutes to seven.

After a while, Léa walked back out, glowing. She put on a happy face—not entirely indicative of what she was feeling in general, but in that moment it was the closest to the truth she had felt in a very long time—and offered her hand to Celeste.

"Shall we go?" Léa said.

Celeste nodded and took her hand.

——

THERE WAS A SINGLE WELL OF LIGHT BEHIND THE apothecary's shop, splashed there from the spherical bowl of a streetlamp. There were rats scurrying about the shadows, and the distant yowling of sick men and women. Theodore Mathieu walked towards it with his hands in his pockets, his shoulders hunched and a white mist tangled inches from his mouth.

Flies buzzed about a trash can. A man stood under the light beside it smoking a cigarette. He wore an impressive coat which billowed around his legs. He spotted Theodore as he approached, and lowered the cigarette. As Theodore drew closer, he found that the mysterious man was wearing what appeared to be an elaborate raven masquerade mask.

"Mister Mathieu," Regis said.

Theodore stopped a short distance away from him, just beyond the ambit of the lamp light. It was so cold he couldn't stop his teeth from chattering. The bells rang throughout the town, signalling seven o'clock.

"My father was called that," Theodore said, trying to keep his voice from shaking. Regis tossed his cigarette onto the ground and it immediately burned up.

"I am sorry about your father," Regis said.

Theodore stepped closer without saying another word.

"My name is Regis. It is true what they say. The headlines. Lady Beaumont murdered your father. I hear you are invited to her ball. Lend me your invitation and I will avenge your father." He pulled aside his coat and revealed a long, curved dagger. Theodore felt his throat tighten as he laid his eyes upon it, sensed something sinister warping off it.

"This dagger murders witches," Regis said.

"Why should I believe you?" Theodore said.

"Why should you believe that what I am saying is true or why should you believe that I'm going to walk straight into her chambers and plunge this dagger into her heart?"

Theodore contemplated the strange man's words. "Both."

"Because I've seen it. The plague. The murders. It's all Lady Beaumont and her witch coven. That's why I'm going to walk in there and kill her. They fear Lady Beaumont but even the most horrifying witch dies when stabbed through the heart, and that is what I will do, even if it kills me. Your father loved this town. He loved France. He would have wanted this."

"I want to see her die," Theodore said, surprised by the heat in his voice.

Regis stepped forward and placed his hand on the Mathieu boy's shoulder. "Your time will come, my boy. Perhaps sooner than you think. But I must do this alone."

Before Theodore knew it, the invitation had exchanged hands and the raven man was walking away through the darkness. Theodore watched him until he disappeared from sight. Only when he was gone did he finally look down at what the raven man had slipped into his grasp: a black feather and a raven masquerade mask, vaguely smeared with blood.

———

LAURENT SIPPED ON A GLASS OF WINE AS HE walked one of the balconies circling the massive and incredible ballroom. He appreciated the music, especially the very handsome conductor, but that was not to say he was a fan of the selection in general. It was a sombre set that the black-clad band was playing and it set him on edge.

He needed to get drunk—and fast. Laurent was a man of control but tonight he could do nothing, at least nothing more than what he'd already done. Tonight his plan unfolded, or it fell apart. He'd already gone through two wine glasses and this was his third. He stood by the railing, nodding respectfully back at a young couple who passed.

He imagined them asking who he was wearing tonight. He would say that it was Louis Vuitton and the vest was expensive, indigo with a faint crisscrossed pattern on it, which he was hoping to be complimented on at least once per hour. The pants were Italian, as were the brown shoes. He was also wearing green spotted socks but those were cheap. His ashen hair was slicked back but imperfectly, so as not to appear too polished. He had shaved before arriving and so his face was as smooth as this golden parapet.

"You should try the Ortolans," Ferdinand said as he returned from his brief reconnaissance through the ballroom. Ferdinand wore a fashionable red coat with gold thread. He offered Laurent an Ortolan meat skewer, which he took and tested.

"This is good meat," he noted.

Ferdinand watched him, then looked around at everybody else. Other candidates walked past and some acknowledged him, but many did not. It was currently four days before the final polls came in, and the final polls were always a good indication of who was claiming the election victory. The night was supposed to be a break from all that, but in the brief moment you met another election candidate's eyes, you were immediately reminded of those forthcoming polls.

"This place often unsettles me," Ferdinand said. "But not tonight."

Laurent agreed half-heartedly and began walking away from Ferdinand, who promptly followed him. He was looking at those servants, remembering how they had all appeared identical on that first day the two had visited Lady Beaumont. He wondered if he would see her tonight. He spotted Yvonne Couture, the younger cousin of Christophe Archambault, standing by a marble pillar. She wore a striking yellow dress and appeared to be looking for somebody.

"Ms. Couture," Laurent said, standing rigid and attentive.

She looked him over. "Laurent. Wonderful to see you. Looking swell as always. How goes your theatre script that you said you were working on?"

"Progress has stalled momentarily."

"A shame. My older cousin despises you but I have always loved your work."

"Thank you. Speaking of Christophe, where is that gross rat?"

Yvonne shrugged, looking around casually and noncommittally. "I was speaking to him earlier but lost him in the crowds. He is likely with some woman."

"Can you tell him something for me?"

Yvonne nodded and Laurent leaned in towards her ear, small and vaguely red from the heat that had at some point during the day become trapped here.

"Tell him to cancel all of his plans because he won't be needing them once he's in jail," Laurent said in one breath without breaking.

Yvonne stared back at him with confusion but Laurent did not stay with her long enough for her to respond. He drank the rest of his wine and placed it on a passing server's tray. He entered a corridor that led to a social room and spotted a woman there who he knew to be a popular performer at the cabaret. She did not look at him, surrounded by other women and a few men, laughing too hard to notice anything else.

Nobody had any reason to suspect anything. Nobody could read this town as well as Laurent. But even if they did suspect that a murder plot was in progress—how could it not be with all those headlines and the murders and the plague and the raven cult and Gustave Mathieu's son?—nobody had planned for it like Laurent had.

He smiled as he walked into the sitting room and observed the gathering campaigners, their made-up wives and families and the rumours spreading from wine-greased tongues. Once Lady Beaumont died, all her influence and power would be transferred to Ferdinand and their party. They already had her endorsement. When Lady Beaumont died, there'd be nobody to hold them accountable. Only chaos could ensue. When that happened, Ferdinand would step in to quell them and reinforce peace, be seen as the protector of Bellvoir. And then before these next four days were up, the votes would pour in and victory was inevitable.

All Laurent had to do now was wait.

"Are you Laurent?" came a voice.

He looked askance to see a young woman in a black dress staring back at him. She had strawberry blonde hair and a very tired face. She couldn't have been a third of his age.

"Excuse me?" he said.

Léa pursed her lips. "Are you the man who was recently endorsed by Lady Beaumont?" She was shaking but not with fear. What did she have to be frightened about? He was only a man. He could do nothing to her.

Laurent straightened. "Yes, that was me."

"I thought so," Léa said as she walked off.

Laurent stared at her until she was gone. Then he shrugged, plucking a few pieces of ham and some crackers from a serving plate and retreating from the room.

CELESTE WALKED THE BALLROOM, GAZING IN wonder at everything in sight. The beautiful dresses and the flavoursome food, all culminating in a perfect aroma of culinary genius. She swayed to the music, narrowly avoiding the dancing couples, and she tried the wine and loved it.

She sat down at a vacant table bordering the dance floor and ate from a platter of various cheeses, her foot tapping along to the beat of the fabulous music.

"That man there, he's a ghost."

She was surprised to find that she was not alone. A man was standing across from her, close enough to hear and yet far enough that she couldn't immediately tell that he was talking to *her*. But he did turn now, staring at her underneath a raven masquerade mask.

His black coat barely moved as he approached, pulled out a seat but did not sit.

"A ghost?" Celeste asked.

Regis nodded, glancing at the conductor. "That's what they say. That's how he's written so many songs. The man has been dead for a long time now, yet he remains alive."

Celeste wondered how such a thing was possible.

"I have seen you around the town," Regis said.

"Have you been watching me?" Celeste asked.

"You were staying at the Lucien estate. That must make you of Lucien blood. Not everything they say about him is true. They wouldn't even know the truth if it stared them in the eye. Have they told you that yet? That Count Lucien murdered people? That he was a misogynistic madman?"

"What?"

"Leave this party."

"Don't talk to her like that," Léa said as she arrived with two glasses of wine. She glared at the man with the raven masquerade mask and felt an immediate chill go through her. The man's expression beneath that mask was difficult to read, blank and monotone.

Regis stared back at this woman and sensed that she was a witch. He became acutely aware of the dagger hidden under the folds of his coat. He looked back and forth between the two women and then walked past them, brushing against Léa.

"Bastard," Léa hissed and Regis ignored it.

CHRISTOPHE ARCHAMBAULT STEPPED OUT OF THE toilets and buttoned up his pants. He spotted his cousin Yvonne walking towards him with an odd look on her face.

"I ran into Laurent," she said.

"What did Laurent say?" Archambault asked absently, already moving past her to drink more wine and look for more women. "Wait, let me guess. Did he say to fuck myself?"

"Something about you going to jail."

This caused Archambault to stop. "Jail for *what*?"

Yvonne shrugged. Archambault snagged a croissant from a serving plate as it flew past his head and immediately chewed into it, crumbs scattering on the carpet. He looked around to see if he could spot Laurent, or the candidate Ferdinand, but neither were in sight. He did see Sophie, his young and attractive mistress talking with some other handsome men.

Then something struck him.

"Wait," he said. "Laurent is here?"

"Is that out of the ordinary?" Yvonne said sceptically.

Archambault immediately forgot about Sophie, forgot about the croissant in his hand to such an extent it slipped between his dirty fingers to the carpet. "Yes," he said.

"Why?" said Yvonne.

"Sophie told me Laurent had flown to Paris."

———

SOPHIE SAW CHRISTOPHE TALKING TO HIS YOUNGER cousin Yvonne and quickly downed the rest of her wine, hurrying from sight. The way he'd looked at her made her tense.

She slipped into the woman's bathroom and slammed the door shut behind her. Inside there, she drew a deep breath and tried to calm down.

Not far from where she was hiding, Laurent had just finished his fourth wine glass and was starting to feel the effects—not that he cared about getting drunk on a perfect night such as this one. And yet all the while he was unaware that his snide comment to Christophe, his greatest of enemies, had just compromised his entire plan, because Sophie, the beautiful woman he had sent to spy on him, had made up an unnecessary lie.

And watching Laurent from just within earshot was Archambault himself, nibbling on the croissant he had picked up off the floor, and he always knew that miscommunication would be Laurent's downfall. So he had sent Sophie to *spy* on him? The bastard!

Archambault always knew he couldn't trust that man, or that wench. He passed Ferdinand as he walked back the way he'd come and grabbed the arm of a woman who wore all black, who he'd seen many times before at the Black Dime Cabaret down the road.

Jacqueline spun around, startled at the tall man. "What?"

"It's Laurent. He's the one who's orchestrating Lady Beaumont's murder." And with that he tossed the girl away and walked off in the complete opposite direction, a smile on his lips.

Jacqueline felt mixed parts confusion and nausea.

Regis passed a smiling Christophe Archambault, wondering what the man was so giddy about. He was unaware that the most powerful man in Bellvoir had just pre-written the headlines and had convinced the public that Laurent was the murderer.

Their political ambitions were dead.

And so when Regis walked to Lady Beaumont's chambers, it was without any heat on his back, without an eye glancing his way. Because it was Laurent, who suddenly feeling quite sick, walked into the men's bathroom across from Sophie in the women's bathroom. It was Laurent who locked himself there and suddenly began to convulse, his limbs twisting erratically, whose screams ripped through the music of the orchestra and whose blood sprayed across every wall. It was Laurent who died first that night and it was Regis who remained unchecked.

JACQUELINE WEPT AS ELEANOR BEAUMONT LET HER leave and she was still crying as Eleanor murdered Laurent with the voodoo doll she had made from him. And now she stood alone in her chambers, having sent Guillaume, her hulking suit of armour, to promptly remove the body. She imagined it to be a horribly impressive sight.

She was now alone.

Regis stood at the doors which hung ajar, peering in. The moonlight through the tinted windows cast a foreboding red glow across the entire chamber. Lady

Beaumont was beautiful. Not even Regis could deny that, and yet he felt that wicked evil seeping off her.

Lady Beaumont had cursed this city. She had created the plague so that the witches could take over. She was murdering election candidates. She would burn down France. Perhaps murdering her would start a revolt. Perhaps Regis *was* to be the tyrant who was born in the gutter. But he knew, in that moment, that there was only one thing that could be done.

He drew the curved dagger and entered her chamber.

She was facing away from him but she knew he had entered.

"Who are you?" Eleanor Beaumont said without looking.

Regis ignored her, the dagger torn from his sheathe, catching the red light that streamed through the windows across the room, splashing them in bloody crimson.

He could not stop. Not pause. He saw nothing, only Lady Beaumont and the plague and the fact that once this was done, everything would go back to normal.

"We have never met but I know you," Eleanor said.

And she did know him. She had seen him in her darkest dreams. She had seen his face in the shadows when there was nothing there to see. The tarot cards spat him out and foretold that he would strike her with a dagger forged in the walls of the institution of Matera in Italy, where Rita Galeazzi was murdered by Count Lucien, who created all this turmoil.

But no, it had not been his face at all.

She had suspected Laurent and she had been wrong.

"France will burn," she said, knowing this for a fact.

But Regis did not stop. Could not stop.

"You are the tyrant who was born in the gutter."

Regis was back inside that chapel with the melodramatic music ringing in the background. He executed the manoeuvre just as he had rehearsed it. He took hold of the dagger, rapidly increased his speed, glided through the air as, at long last, he lashed out at her.

Eleanor turned just as he did this, gripping the dagger's blade and feeling pain erupt through her body. She screamed, forcing the dagger away from her. Regis howled, tightening his grip around it, grabbing her shoulder in his hand.

"Please!" Eleanor cried as she crumpled to one knee.

Regis roared, ripping the dagger free with such force it tore her palm in half, splitting the tendons with a ferocious screech. Her eyes widened as he stabbed the dagger straight through her heart. Eleanor croaked, coughing out blood. Regis held her as she went limp, blood squirting out of her punctured heart and splashing on the carpet.

A tear rolled down the side of her face.

Regis pulled out the dagger and stabbed her again. She gave a croak, red lips parting as if to speak, but no words came. Her eyes glazed over and she sagged in his arms, no sign of life inside her. Regis ripped out the dagger and tossed her onto the floor like dirt, standing up and drawing heavy breaths, emotion stripped from him.

Léa was standing near Guillaume when it happened. She immediately knew. It was a feeling that not only struck her entire body but caused the whole world to tilt on its side, as every inch of air turned painfully cold. It was as clear as if somebody had screamed it into her ear. Lady Beaumont was dead. And she knew that Guillaume knew it too.

The Lady's hound sprinted to her chambers.

"I don't feel so good," Celeste said. She had gone deathly pale. Léa felt heat streak through her veins. "Then go," she spat. "Go back home, Celeste. Please." Celeste stared back at her, not quite sure what to do, what to say. She had drunk too much wine and she felt dizzy, the ballroom spinning. She felt hot. She wanted to be violently sick.

Léa stormed from the house of Eleanor Beaumont.

A man who was trapped in a clown's outfit sat atop a roof smoking a cigar, the house of Eleanor Beaumont in the distance. He knew what had happened.

He had failed.

X

THE BURNING OF BELLVOIR

 aria?" André ascended the stairs into Maria's room, the black cat Clotilde watching him from the other side, behind a fold in the pink curtains. "Maria?"

His eyes widened and he dropped the plate he'd been holding. Ceramic, potatoes and vegetables crashed to the floor. He just about screamed, but something choked him. Maria was not in her bed. She was not in her wheelchair.

Maria was standing by the window.

Standing! She had not done that in decades!

Wind howled through the open window, snagging at the curtain and sending it streaming around her.

The cat darted from the spot, ducking between Maria's legs and hiding on the other side of the room. Maria's stained white nightgown seemed even more dreadful now illuminated by the moonlight. Her pale arms with its sagging skin and protruding bones gave her the horrible appearance of a ghoul. She was as folded as a hunchback.

"Maria, what are you doing?" André gasped.

"Eleanor has died," Maria said.

"What?" He slowly approached her, delicate with his movements. Maria's crooked, haggard shadow bathed him as she became silhouetted by the lights outside. She began to weep and then she became hysterical.

"I can't see anything, André!" she bellowed.

"It's okay," he responded, taking her hand and wrapping his other arm around her. "How about you come back to bed?" His voice was trembling and he felt suddenly ill. "Maria, please. You should not be out of bed."

Maria screamed. It was the most horrible sound André had ever heard, so horrible indeed that he immediately screamed himself and flew from her, grasping his chest. Urine dribbled down Maria's leg, thick and yellow. "God have mercy on us!"

"What are you doing?" André whimpered.

She ran forward and jumped out the window.

"MARIA!" André screamed.

Her body smashed the cobbles with the sound of shattering bones. Blood splashed across the road, chips of bone exploding upon impact and showering everything in sight. Back inside the house, André collapsed to the floor with his hands over his head, and the black cat watched him, afraid of what would come next.

GUILLAUME SMASHED DOWN THE DOOR INTO LADY Beaumont's chambers and saw only her blood-drenched body on the carpet, and an open window leading out to the moon.

He roared, running over to her dead body and cradling it in his arms. She was limp, blood dripping onto Guillaume's rusted metal armour. A universe exploded inside him, the sound deafening, clutching her as tight as possible, so tight that her body became bruised with the pressure of it against his armour.

Guillaume knew only one thing: murder. He gently placed down Lady Beaumont's body and rushed to the open window, drawing his broadsword. It hissed as it sailed through the air and landed in his grasp.

Curtains blew against the breeze above the long drop, which ended on the rooftop of another smaller building, then trees. Guillaume knew only one thing: the man who murdered Lady Beaumont had escaped through this window and was getting away. That man needed to die.

Voices exploded from behind him.

"What has happened?" one screamed.

"Oh my god!" came another.

Guillaume howled, jumping out the window and landing on the cobbles, which cracked underneath his metal feet. He did not stumble. Simply grasped his broadsword in one massive hand and followed where his instincts led him, through the dark street.

———

REGIS JUMPED ONTO A TABLE IN THE BAR AND raised a glass of beer to the ceiling. The table creaked underneath his weight. Coins rattled and clattered to the floor. "Lady Midnight is dead!" he pronounced, her blood dripping from his coat.

Three men in raven masks were standing at the back of the bar, watching him. They wore pistols in their belts. Standing in the doorway was Gustave Mathieu's son, Theodore, also wearing one of those masks. He watched the raven man with mixed parts disbelief and amazement. You could not kill Lady Midnight, and yet he had, and all of a sudden his father was avenged and the witch was fucking dead!

"Lady Midnight is dead!" Regis bellowed.

People cheered and the ground rumbled and dust fell from the rafters into their drinks, but nobody cared—they just kept drinking because Lady Midnight was dead.

"My brethren," Regis said now in a calmer tone of voice, standing in a sea of angry people in a bar not far from the house of Lady Beaumont. "The witch queen has been murdered and now all who serve in her shadow are vulnerable. Witches live among us! Hear me! Witches live among us and they caused the plague that's eating up the poor and unfortunate in the gutter! And when all the miserable are dead, the witches will come for you! See this! Witches murdered election candidate Gustave Mathieu and left his son without a father!"

Regis looked to Theodore. "Come here, boy!"

Theodore found himself walking over to Regis without even thinking about it, the cheers around him igniting a fire inside his stomach. From his coat, Regis withdrew a bloody, curved dagger, soaked in so much blood it created a crimson mirror in which Theodore could see his own face, the raven masquerade mask hiding the storm of emotions he was feeling. Fear, in some way, but more than fear it was hatred for the witches, and determination.

Opportunity.

Regis extended the haft of the dagger to him. Theodore looked up at him, paralysed. Power warped off this man, a power that was only amplified by the crowd.

"This dagger murders witches," Regis said.

Theodore took it, examined the bloodthirsty steel. His heart was pounding so hard he thought he might start coughing up blood but he remained headstrong as he gazed at the swirling crowd. They were singing that Lady Midnight had been murdered, singing about the plague and the murders and the horrible witches in Bellvoir.

Theodore raised the dagger. "Death to all witches!"

The crowd screamed with hungry ferocity. Torches were lit. Alcohol turned into bombs. Fire shrieked into existence and angry screams became howls and taunts. Regis and Theodore stood amongst it, the other raven men watching without speaking a word.

"The witches congregate at the Black Dime Cabaret!" Regis screamed. "Tonight they hide in fear. Bellvoir is no place for witches, is what I say! Hear me!

Make them sing for you tonight a song of death! Make the witches cry! Make them disappear off the face of the Earth!"

Rats squawked and ravens flew into the night sky as the doors of the bar were blasted open and the raven's mob descended upon the streets. Torches burned holes in the night. Hollers and taunts soured the air. Regis jumped from the table and gripped young Theodore's shoulder. Regis was not afraid anymore. He was not afraid now that Lady Midnight was dead and the mob was on the hunt. "Go forth and murder them," Regis said.

Theodore felt nothing but admiration for the raven man. He gripped the bloodstained dagger in his hand—blood from Lady Midnight herself—and walked out the doors of the bar into the night. Regis watched him. His raven followers congregated around him.

"Spread the word," he said. "The witch queen is dead."

ARCHAMBAULT FLED ONTO THE STREET, ALREADY hopelessly out of breath. "What the hell is going on?" he whispered as the angry mob appeared. He grabbed his tie and ripped it off, popping a few buttons of his shirt just so he could breathe.

Eleanor Beaumont is dead, was all he could think of, rushing through the frantic crowds in order to get back to the office and start writing tomorrow's headlines. News like this only ever came about once in a lifetime and he would not miss the opportunity to break it.

He stumbled as he rounded a corner into the courtyard outside the offices. He took this moment to catch his breath, slowing down to a walk.

"Constant!" he shouted, trying to get the attention of somebody.

Somebody appeared but it was not Constant. The dark figure approached him across the street, eventually resolving into the form of a woman in a black dress.

"Who's there?" Archambault said. "Is that you, Sophie?"

Something gripped his spine and twisted it violently. He screamed as his back contorted and he landed on the ground. "Help!" he screamed. "Witch! There's a *fucking witch*!"

Léa strode over to him, twisting harder in her mind's eye. Archambault quivered, cursing as his spine *cracked*. He screamed, tears shooting from his wide-open eyes, his arms splaying through the air. He tried to get up but something was crushing him from within, immobilising him.

"HOLY SHIT!" Archambault wailed.

The light from a streetlamp fleshed out Léa as she stood over him, her black dress swirling about erratically. The sounds of chanting and shouting became just a rumble in the back of her mind, and at the forefront of everything appeared Archambault. His face was contorted in the most horrible expression she had ever seen, blood dribbling out of his nose. He reached out to her in much the same way a drowning man grapples for a raft.

She forced him to stand, puppeteering him using the techniques that had been written in Count Lucien's book all those years ago, magic which had been forgotten in time for only two copies of the book had ever been published, and she had been taught from one of them.

Archambault's body moved by its own accord until he was suspended in the air, his neck and spine at odd angles, forced to stare up into the witch's eyes. His heartbeat thumped loudly in his ears, his breath uneven, his body aching. The woman stared at him with dagger eyes, her black mascara accentuating the thirst for death that swelled inside them.

"I haven't done anything!" Archambault croaked.

"Who did this? Who fucking killed her?"

Archambault smiled and began to laugh. "I didn't do anything!"

Léa snapped his arm in half so that the bone speared out his elbow. He shrieked and gave a hideous yowl as she threw him onto the cobbles, dirt and rats scurrying about him.

"Oh god!" Archambault cried.

Léa slammed him into the lamppost with such force it shattered, trickling glass on top of his broken body. Archambault lay there, twitching, unable to move for his body had been annihilated. All he could do was laugh and watch the witch approach him for the last time. "You did this!" Léa screamed, pulling out a knife. "You and your fucking headlines! You and your fucking newspapers! Your rumours! Your lies! *Everything!* You're the reason this has happened!"

Archambault chuckled. "And was I wrong?"

"You lied about everything just so you could hurt her!"

"I said there are witches in Bellvoir! And here you are! Where's the lie in that?"

Léa piffed the knife through his skull and Christophe Archambault was dead.

Wiping tears from her eyes, she turned to see the shadows of the lynch mob marching through the streets, heard their shouts and their songs, smelt the smoke of their flames. She had to find Celeste. She had to get back to the cabaret and tell Marguerite what was happening. Everything was wrong. Everything was falling apart.

They were no longer safe here.

———

JACQUELINE THREW OPEN THE DOOR INTO THE Black Dime Cabaret and slammed it shut behind her. The cabaret bar was empty except for Marguerite, who was sitting at a table drinking.

"Marguerite!" Jacqueline cried, rushing forward through the pink lights towards her. Marguerite looked up with the same expression she had worn earlier.

"You must not be here," Marguerite said sternly.

"They killed her," Jacqueline said, tears streaming down her face.

"They will come here next."

"There's a mob of them. They're burning down this town, killing us for no reason at all. We haven't done anything and yet they're coming to kill us. What do we do?"

Marguerite stared at her with a frightened but unsurprised expression. The two had spoken earlier in the room side of stage, just the two of them. Marguerite had asked about Léa and Jacqueline had told her everything, about the people who hated witches and that Léa was going to do something bad because she felt like she had no choice, and Marguerite had said that perhaps Bellvoir was no place for witches anymore, and maybe it wasn't up to them.

Marguerite walked to Jacqueline and held her hands.

"Find as many of us as you can," she said, "including Celeste and your brother and Léa and anybody else you can find, and then find this man." She offered a slip of creased paper with a single name and address on it. "This man is a sailor and he has multiple ships. If you can go to him, he will take you aboard his next vessel south down the river."

Jacqueline stared at the name on the paper.

"He owes me a debt for something that happened long ago," Marguerite said, staring at the slip of paper and wondering how long it had been since the two of them had spoken in person. Probably way too long. She closed Jacqueline's small, cold hand around the slip of paper and then stared straight into her eyes. "You must go, Jacqueline."

"What about you?" she asked.

"There's no life for me beyond the cabaret."

Jacqueline gripped her hands tighter as a guttural shout erupted outside and the ground began to rumble with the energy of hundreds of stamping feet. "Please come!"

Marguerite smiled reassuringly. "By all means, then. Stay." She walked away and stared out the window at the approaching hurricane of fire. "I think I'm going to watch the fireworks."

"I can't do it by myself," Jacqueline pleaded.

Marguerite turned. "Of course you can. You're a witch, aren't you?"

Jacqueline thought about this, thought about all of it, how she now stood in the centre of everything, that the fate of all the witches in Bellvoir depended on her getting them to this man's boat and sailing south down the river.

She nodded. "I *am* a witch."

"Then walk through that door out the back and find the others."

"I love you, Marguerite," Jacqueline said.

"That's why you must leave me."

Marguerite waited until Jacqueline was gone and she was the last one inside the Black Dime Cabaret. She lit a cigarette and smoked it as she walked to the phonograph and turned it on. Her favourite symphony oozed seductively through the horn. Hector Berlioz's *Symphonie Fantastique*. She let the beautiful melodies of its final movement fill the Black Dime Cabaret.

Outside, a man in a raven mask threw a torch against the cabaret walls and they erupted into flames. The arched windows lit up with shocking exuberance. Marguerite stood there in the middle of the bar, staring at the wild flames.

"Death to all witches!" someone screamed.

There was an explosion of fire and the Black Dime Cabaret became engulfed in it. The wooden sign caught, falling to the cobbles where it burned away into oblivion. The red glass windows caught aflame and spontaneously exploded. Marguerite squinted at the fire as it chewed up the floorboards and the bar and the tables.

She took a drag of her cigarette.

Such a shame, she thought as the ceiling began to collapse and fire lit up the floorboards around her. She blew out a breath of smoke. *I had such incredible plans.*

And then the Black Dime Cabaret collapsed.

JACQUELINE RAN FASTER THAN SHE HAD EVER RUN before through the streets of Bellvoir. There was the most frightening shriek of fire behind her and the air grew hot as the Black Dime Cabaret burst into flames, lighting up this horrible, horrible night.

She stopped in an alleyway to catch her breath, wiping tears from her eyes and sweat from her face, smudging her perfectly-done makeup.

"This can't be happening," she murmured. It was so dark, the air thick with smoke. She grabbed the cold brick wall of the alley and used it to keep her balance as she kept going. "Léa!" she screamed. "Vincent!"

Please don't be dead, she prayed. *Please don't be dead...*

A dark figure in a raven mask appeared at the other end of the alleyway. Jacqueline froze, rooted to the spot. The man pulled out a long dagger and approached her, firelight flickering against him from above. "Witch!" he bellowed.

"Wait," Jacqueline gasped.

"You'll all burn for this!" Theodore Mathieu growled.

He was sprinting. A gunshot rang out and he dropped to the ground, the curved dagger flying from his grasp and spinning away across the cobbles. Jacqueline jumped, cowering from the echoing gunshot. Theodore peeled himself off the ground, blood gushing from his shoulder. He collected the dagger and jumped to his feet but a second gunshot cracked. The bullet struck his other shoulder, taking off a chunk of flesh.

Jacqueline spun around to see the man with the pistol standing behind her, thin white smoke rising from the hot barrel. "Who are you?" she whispered.

The man who stepped out of the shadows wore a large red coat with gaudy gold buttons and expensive thread. His hair was too long and his beard uneven. "Don't worry about it," he said in a thick baritone voice, the pistol still aimed at the twitching man on the ground.

Ferdinand didn't know what he was doing helping this witch but he knew that he had to. This was never meant to happen. Bellvoir was never meant to burn. Witches were never meant to die. But he knew that he had played a part in it and that was enough to persuade him to do something. "Where do you need to get to?" Ferdinand said.

"The harbour," Jacqueline said.

Ferdinand nodded and started down the alley, Jacqueline in his wake. Theodore groaned, attempting to climb back onto his feet. Ferdinand stood over him.

"Foolish boy," he said. "Go back to your family. They need you."

Theodore stared up at him, reaching for his foot but Ferdinand kicked out, striking him in the jaw. "Don't touch me. Your father would be ashamed if he saw you now." Theodore curled up into a ball. Jacqueline stared at him, feeling anger surge through her. She wanted to spit on him, wanted to scream at him and demand why they were doing this, but she remained silent.

Ferdinand looked back at her. "Let's round up who we can and get you out of here."

THE CLOWN WATCHED THE BLACK DIME CABARET burn from a distance, a cigarette poking out from between his red lips, his pale makeup becoming embalmed with the light from the flames. Bellvoir ran hot with the sound of screams and shouts.

Rats darted through the beams of light, nibbling on the dead bodies that lay on the streets. Plague-infected sick wandered from the lower districts with their naked emaciated frames, wondering who had come to save them. Lady Beaumont was dead.

Everybody knew it. The witches were under attack. The clown could do nothing about it.

He saw Celeste Lucien stumble through the smoke and lose her footing, collapsing on hands and knees. He observed her carefully, drifting from the spot so he could be nearer to her, blowing a puff of smoke into the wind.

Celeste climbed to her feet and sucked in a deep breath. A wall of fire loomed before her, as intimidating as a wave that was about to crash into a rowboat. It was so intense that she couldn't keep her eyes open, felt the backs of her eyelids catching fire. Her head was spinning as she crashed into the crooked bole of a tree, autumn leaves hailing across her. People were screaming all around her, bombarding her with noise and sensations and overwhelming pain.

This is a nightmare, she told herself.

Please let it be a nightmare . . .

She collapsed onto a wooden bench and vomited all over the ground, thick and red. She wiped her mouth and caught spots of black rot on her arm. Rats squeaked at her feet, nibbling through her dress to her skin.

She was alone—as alone as she'd been since the war.

Alone but for the clown, who slowly approached her in the shadows.

Celeste closed her eyes and everything became much more quiet. She heard a voice in the back of her mind, a friendly and familiar voice which she eventually recognised as belonging to Maria. *It is okay,* she said inside her mind. *You can let go now. We have you.*

She opened her eyes and stood up, holding onto the back of the bench for support. The world tilted on its side and she saw the clown standing in the distance, staring back at her. He seemed so close and yet so far away, as if separated by time itself. She reached out to him but something else grabbed her arm, something sharp and bony and tough, and it yanked her forward.

She screamed as the air split open and she fell into absolute darkness.

Suspended in an endless puddle of nothing, specks of white dust floating around her, blinking in and out of existence. Embers floated through the air like tiny red eyes. She spun head over heels in slow motion, not breathing but finding that she didn't need to breathe.

Her lungs were the universe.

"CELESTE." The voice came from a single shape in the distance, which she was steadily drifting towards. "CELESTE LUCIEN." The voice was amplified, as if every speck of matter were a microphone. She eventually slowed to a stop and the figure stood up from wherever he was sitting, walking through the abyss towards her, a man with a skeleton's face.

Celeste stared at him, not blinking.

The creature offered her his hand. "COME."

"Who are you?" she asked but her voice was not her own.

"DANCE WITH ME. AND WE CAN TALK ABOUT EVERYTHING."

Celeste had stopped floating, now inches away from the man with the skeleton face who only vaguely resembled a man. He took her hand carefully and smiled. As she stopped floating, her dress ensnared them, becoming a cosmic whirlpool.

Death smiled. "SHALL WE?"

And with that, he took her where only the dead could go.

TO BE CONTINUED IN . . .
"THE PHANTOM BALLET"

1959

an excerpt from

"Reflections of Fontaine"

My breaths are echoed by something outside of my own body, but at a quarter to four a.m. there's nothing, just the snow. I'm watching it sizzle against the tip of my cigarette like hot whispers on a cold winter's night. Beyond this, the words **Paris, 1959** shine in the storm clouds, a classic titles sequence. The score is Bernard Herrmann.

The reviews will be *stellar*.

I watch the darkness gush through Paris as floodwater does when poured through a miniature town. It splashes thick and nebulous across the brick buildings and lamp posts, strangling their meagre yellow lights. I've grown to enjoy this. The all-engulfing darkness. The quiet. I continue to chew on the end of my cigarette, bitter and wet.

There's something about this city at night and you can't quite capture it in a cartoon strip in the *Canard*. The monochrome palette, the repetitive blizzard winds, over and over and over, the drunkards moaning on sidewalks and the leftover music tiptoeing out dead-hour establishments. How to spin a feeling into something tangible. It's the snow, it's the fumes, it's the booze stuck against the sidewalk—well, it's booze or vomit.

I take a drag of my cigarette and feel the city suck in a breath too.

Yellow headlights catch me as I exhale smoke into the air, dropping the cigarette to the tips of my fingers and letting it dangle by my side. Staring through the yellow haze, I can vaguely make out the face of the car's sole occupant, a middle-aged man with a clean shave and large red ears. If you asked me, I'd imagine his ears are red because of the weather and not because of some disease of the skin, but who can be sure. This is the fifties, isn't it, and there's a lot to be shared around in times like these.

The man isn't looking at me because he's peering around at the parking signs, all bent like they're puking out the snow. You can't make out a single thing they say, but who's checking where cars are parked at four a.m. amidst a storm like this.

The car engine goes silent, the headlights vanish in a gasp, and the door clicks open. I shiver as the city gives out a tremble that sounds like brass.

The city freezes frame and the words **Nicolas Fontaine** flash against the skyline, like the beginning of a Hitchcockian thriller. There's smoke in the air, gone morbidly rigid; and a woman's silhouette through her frosted window, fingers gripping the curtain, watching the car, watching me. I look up and she disappears behind a curtsy of fabric.

The large man exits his vehicle, one stocky leg kicking out with theatrics, and then the other. He wears black business pants and glossy shoes, and his suit jacket is congruously black and professional. From the darkness he withdraws a satin hat and slaps it on his horribly-balding head. Then the car door swings shut, scraping the snow-covered footpath with the sound smokers make when they snore.

The Fat Man.

This is all I can glean from him as he locks his car door with a jangle of keys, then walks underneath the streetlamp beside mine, throwing his swollen hands into his pockets. The only thing that marks him as anything besides ordinary is the simple fact he's out so early and he's here in front of me. I continue to watch him as I let the cigarette sail from my fingertips and land in the snow, the burning end face-up like an industrial tower pissing smoke.

"Good night," says the fat man.

His voice alarms me. Baritone and sleepy, it's as if you crossed the singer Distel, and Constantine from the *Lemmy Caution* films, rolling out of bed. I gaze at the frost vapour oozing out of the fat man's fat lips, and suddenly I'm struck with the urge to draw him. He is not a particularly short man but his voluminous suit jacket gives the illusion of stout legs. His top hat speckled with frost provides comical height. My above-average olfactory glands can't smell anything besides Paris, but I'd imagine his hat carries the stench of dirty backseats.

The fat man's eyes lift, peering at me ponderously.

"What," I ask in an unpunctuated tone.

The winds howl in response and the fat man clutches the brim of his hat.

"I said *good night*," the fat man repeats. He walks closer with his hands outlined through his pockets, disappearing in the dimness between the two streetlamps, then reappearing in the ambit of mine. He has good skin for a fat man, clean and unblemished.

Finally, he stops. "What did ya think of the show, then?"

The lamp we're standing under burns out, and then flickers back on again, suddenly accentuating the frost that's gathering on the fat man's bushy brows.

Now that he mentions it, I don't remember much about the show, but my fingers scour my coat pocket instinctively and brush up against a cold ticket stub, which is flimsy and small.

"You got a problem hearing me, boy? Eh? The show's what I'm talking about, the one down at the theatre just two blocks out. You were there, weren't ya? Now no use lyin' about things yet."

It's hard to notice a city during the day, when the streets run hot with car fumes and choking exhausts and thrumming engines, but on nights such as this one, an ordinary night in February 1959, even despite the blizzard, you notice it.

For example, the city snickers.

"Have you been following me," I say.

The fat man glides closer still, his head moving through his most recent gasp of frost. Our close proximity exposes his lack of any substantial height and I find myself almost face-to-face with his top hat. He steps up onto the tips of his toes and says, "Not following you. Just paying attention."

He looks at me as if that is any reasonable response.

"How do you know who I am," I say to him.

"I asked at the laundromat," says the fat man.

"I don't work down there anymore."

"Takes more than a resignation to make a person disappear."

There's a sudden cramp in my chest, the kind that conjures the thought, *I couldn't be having a heart attack, I'm only twenty-five,* and yet the thought passes my head nonetheless. Did I lose consciousness sometime during the night. It would explain why I can't remember the show, for one.

My hands are riffling my coat for another cigarette. It finally appears in my right hand, lighter in my left. *Snap. Hiss. Sizzle.* There's a brief spark of amber. Smoke belly-dances in front of my face as I light the cigarette.

I focus on the fat man, who makes a sound between a cough and a chortle, like a man choking on a really good burger. He's staring back at me through a sheet of falling snow. If you listened now, you'd hear the scuff of tires on frost-slick roads, of a dog barking across the street, then abruptly stop, as if sensing something in the air had changed.

"Where are my manners, then?" says the fat man in his dulcet voice. "I'm a representative from a corporation currently testing a new kind of **drug**. We're looking for participants in a brief trial and your name came up as a potential candidate. Have you ever signed up for anything like this? Been asked, ya lookin' for a way to earn quick money? That's probably how we found you in the first place." A slip of paper crinkles against my fingertips. I clutch it involuntarily. I'm staring over the fat man's shoulder down the deserted sidewalk, where one of the streetlamps is turning on and off like morse code. I can feel the fat man's warm breaths reach my neck.

He keeps his voice low and baritone. "I've slipped a piece of paper into your hand. On this piece of paper is a number, and if you dial that number you will speak to a man who sounds like a woman but I assure you, he is not a woman, that's just his voice. This man will put you into contact with another man, and this man will ask you a question, and if you answer this question correctly, you'll wake up the next morning to find one hundred fifty francs in your bank account." He shrinks down to his usual, below-average height and looks at me.

"What do you want with a failed cartoonist," I ask him.

"As the lottery chooses its winner," the fat man says, "Moscati Research has chosen you." Despite this, I sense things aren't so straightforward, and this is no simple lottery.

"Moscati Research. What the hell is that."

"Moscati Research Laboratories is one of the pioneering forces in scientific development in the twentieth century," says the fat man. "I have slipped you a piece of paper with a number on it. Once you speak to the man on the other end, you will learn more."

I remain silent. I don't recall ever putting my name down for something like this, but all things considered, I don't trust my memory so much tonight. All I can think of is that I used to pop one every now and then, but then again, how would the fat man know this; and besides, it's not been for some time. There's no other reason why I'm being approached except that it's a con, and it certainly sounds like one. But the look the fat man gives me suggests he's not playing around, and why did he come looking for me at the laundromat.

The snowing winds suddenly change direction, like a man walking through a grocery store he has never been in before. I become aware of the warmth that a human body gives when its standing nearby another, but at the same time goose bumps spring up on my arms. I think about the fat man's words, and about the piece of paper enclosed within my cold fingers. There's not enough space between us for any snow to fall.

"What was the show," I find myself asking.

The fat man smiles without teeth. I search his eyes for some sign of anything, but it's like staring into a puddle of trodden-over mud. "Marcel Aymé's *A View from the Bridge*," he says matter-of-factly, frost flying from his mouth. "You ever thought about going to America, Nicolas?"

"Wait a minute, how do you know my name."

"I told you, I asked at the laundromat where you no longer work, but like I also said, it's not so easy to disappear completely."

"Oh."

The fat man makes a hmph noise, but it could just be a bit of food stuck in his throat, rather than much consideration for anything in particular. "I've heard it's nice over there. America. They have all the good movies, don't they."

I have no answer to this. So, without another word, the fat man turns and leaves. All that's left is the spitting of snow through the space where he had been.

I shiver, clutching the piece of paper and thinking about *A View from the Bridge*, not that I can remember much from it, pieces of the night censored and forgotten.

The fat man inserts a key into his car door, then climbs in and turns on the ignition. Headlights drench me in hot mustard and I squint, lifting a hand to shield my eyes. Slowly, the car rolls forward until it's side-by-side with me.

The window rolls down clumsily.

"It's just a bit *old-fashioned* isn't it, the theatre," the fat man says, directly quoting something I wrote for the *Canard* maybe three months or so ago. His eyes look askance but his smile stays where it is. He's lit a cigarette and he perches it on the edge of his mouth. "I liked your cartoons, Nicolas. Very progressive." He looks back at me—

"Now how the hell'd you end up gettin' like this?"

I stare at the fat man until the tinted window chomps him up. Wheels screech in the snow and the car disappears up the road, and I'm thinking about the show that I can't remember, and I'm thinking about what the fat man has told me.

For the first time tonight, I lift the piece of paper in my hand. The left edge is crone's teeth jagged, like torn from a lined notebook. The phone number has been written in blue pen, obtrusively smudged from the snow. As my phone line was recently disconnected, I don't currently have access to one directly, but there's a booth about twenty metres down the road. I glance at it now, covered in frost.

I look back down at the phone number scribbled in blue. By all accounts, ordinary. According to the fat man, if I dial this number there will be a man who sounds like a woman, and then there will be another man who asks me a question. I wonder what sort of question he will ask me.

But if I answer correctly, they'll pay me one hundred fifty francs, which, times as they are, is decent money. Far more than a few days' work at the laundromat.

A strange sense of unjudgmental calm comes over me, and I throw the piece of paper onto the ground. Like rats that are hungry, the snow opens up its maws and engulfs it. I kick it with my boot to be sure, and sure enough it's gone. The cigarette I left there, still sizzling with faint amber, also vanishes under the ravenous snowbank.

At last, with hands in my trouser pockets, I walk away.

In a band room deep down in the catacombs of Paris, one February night in 1959, or a morning, if you have some place to be, a trumpet vomits notes into the city air, and the rest of the band splashes around in it, turning it into music.

I look up as white text dissolves into the air.

It's the title of a film, superimposed over the darkened sky, untouched by the frost and the streetlamps. Synthetic white text, the font simplistic, *Clarendon* or *Aldine*.

Reflections of Fontaine is what it says.

Follow Black Dime Cabaret

@blackdimecabaret

on Instagram, TikTok, YouTube and Facebook

or visit
www.blackdimecabaret.com
for more!

Black Dime Cabaret is

Caitlyn Adshead
Brandon Young
Patrick Ng
Luke Bosnich
Joel Holdsworth

*Listen to our music now
on a streaming service near you!*